THE DESERTER TROOP

Also by the Author

THE DESERTER TROOP

Jack Cummings

Walker and Company
New York

First published in the United States of America in 1991 by Walker Publishing Company, Inc.

Published simultaneously in Canada by Thomas Allen & Son Canada, Limited, Markham, Ontario

Library of Congress Cataloging-in-Publication Data

Cummings, Jack, 1925–
The deserter troop / Jack Cummings.
p.   cm.
ISBN 0-8027-4121-5
I. Title.
PS3553.U444D45   1991
813'.54—dc20   91-16872
CIP

Printed in the United States of America

2   4   6   8   10   9   7   5   3   1

CONTENTS

Author's Note

In the frontier U.S. Army, the elimination of cruel and unusual punishment for enlisted men was long in coming.

Although flogging had been abolished by General Order No. 54 in 1864, it was not until the Act of June 6, 1872, that it was made illegal to brand the body of a soldier by sentence of a court-martial.

That act came two months too late to save Private Raymond Craig from his fate.

THE DESERTER TROOP

PROLOGUE

Arizona Territory, April 1872

Fort Maxon was a one-troop station, a small outpost on the far northwest edge of the army's effort to contain the Tonto Apache threat that lurked beyond the surrounding mesquite and cactus and creosote bush.

It was garrisoned by Troop D, First United States Cavalry.

The troop was a short company of a scant fifty men of the seventy-eight authorized by the Tables of Organization.

On this morning the troop was in dress uniform, waiting in special formation before the weathered-board post headquarters. The troop's commanding officer, Lieutenant Charles Arnett, stood in front, followed by First Sergeant Joe Madden. Beside him were two guards and a prisoner.

Facing the troop was the post commander, Captain Brandon Falk.

Lieutenant Arnett, grim-faced, saluted Falk and said, "Sir, all present and accounted for."

Captain Falk returned the salute, then drew from his tunic a sheet of paper and began to read:

"From Headquarters, Department of Arizona: Of the General Court-Martial of Private Raymond Craig, Company D, First United States Cavalry:

For disobeying the orders of his troop commander to carry expeditiously a message to his post that his detach-

1

ment was in dire need of reinforcements when surrounded by a vastly greater force of enemy Apaches, in fact to have abandoned temporarily his mission in contradiction of said orders, thus being guilty of desertion and dereliction of duty that caused additional wounded casualties among his comrades, Private Raymond Craig is hereby sentenced to be formally degraded before company formation by the stripping from his uniform of all marks and insignia of his unit and of the Army.

He is furthermore sentenced to be branded on both hips with the capital letter D, officially recognized as the mark of a deserter, and to be dishonorably discharged from the United States Army and escorted from his assigned post."

Lieutenant Arnett kept his eyes front on Falk, controlling an urge to glance to his left where twenty-two-year-old Private Craig stood stiffly, held by a guard on either side.

"Lieutenant," Captain Falk said, "administer the sentence of the court."

Arnett stepped over to where the prisoner stood. He took out a pocket knife, opened it, and commenced cutting away the brass insignia from Private Craig's uniform, the crossed sabers from the collar first, then each button down the front of the tunic.

Finished, he turned to address First Sergeant Madden. "Sergeant, bring up the farrier."

"Yes, sir." Madden passed the order to the rear.

The farrier came forward, carrying a bucket of hot coals in one hand, a pair of iron tongs and a small hand bellows in the other.

He set down the bucket and with the bellows brought the coals to a red heat. He then dropped the bellows, picked up the tongs, and plucked from the coals a reddened harness D ring.

Arnett turned to the guards. "Strip down his trousers," he said. "And hold him tight."

The farrier said, "Ready, sir?"

"Do it," the lieutenant said, his face held to a mask.

"Which hip first, sir?" the farrier said.

"Dammit, man! Does it matter?"

"Yes, sir," the farrier said, and pressed the scorching D ring against the white skin of Private Craig's hip, expecting a cry of agony.

It did not come.

There was no sound either from the assembled troopers.

There was only the quick, faint sizzle of frying flesh, and the smoke and the smell.

The guards turned the prisoner to present the other hip. This time, when the iron seared him, a strangled cry came from his throat.

The lieutenant jerked his eyes away from the branding, looked over at Captain Falk, saw the look of satisfaction on Falk's face, and gave a silent curse.

The son of a bitch enjoys this, he thought.

First Sergeant Joe Madden also noticed the captain's sadistic pleasure, but instead of cursing the commander, he saw this as an opportunity. Falk's actions would make it easier for Madden to pick the men he wanted from the witnessing troopers.

Men for a campaign of his own.

PART I
Desertion

CHAPTER 1

WHEN Private Craig saw Captain Falk's look of satisfaction, he cursed himself silently for not repressing the faint cry that had escaped him.

A young man not inclined to show pain, Craig now stood erect and stared at the face of the post commander, keeping his torment to himself.

Captain Falk was a harsh disciplinarian, an officer unwilling to forgive a breach of orders, no matter what the extenuating circumstances.

He was not a forgiving man toward any of his command. An iron-assed tyrant, forged in the furnace of the War Between the States, Falk still harbored a prejudice against all southerners, even seven years after Appomattox. And it was Craig's—a Virginian—misfortune to be in Falk's command.

It did not matter to Falk that Craig was too young to have served in the war.

A more humane commander might have responded more leniently to Private Craig's error of judgment. After all, Craig had acted instinctively to save a child's life. Even though his express orders were to ride for the fort, letting *nothing* delay him.

As Falk had just described in reading the special order of his court-martial, Craig *had* gotten himself delayed. He had been a third of the way to the post when he topped a rise and saw a pair of Apache braves at the site of a halted wagon.

At first, Craig thought to swing wide of them, since he apparently had not been seen by them. Then he saw the fallen inert forms of the two whites, by their dress a man and a woman, arrows still protruding from their bodies. The Apaches, knives in hand, were further mutilating them.

Still, he would have tried to avoid discovery, mindful of his orders, until he saw the small boy sitting on the seat of the wagon, wailing. He saw one of the Apaches turn from the corpses, stride to the child, grab him off the seat, and swing him by the ankles, ready to smash his head against a wheel.

Without thought, and beyond effective revolver range, Craig drew his holstered handgun and fired a shot, spurring his mount in a direct charge toward them.

The Apache dropped the child and grabbed a rifle from the ground, even as his companion did likewise.

One of them fired. And missed.

Craig was upon them, firing from the back of his plunging mount. And not missing. He had a fine talent with a handgun.

But the final exchange with the surviving brave brought a bullet that creased Craig's scalp and brought black oblivion to him.

He regained consciousness much later to find the child dead, pierced by a bullet, ostensibly fired in a last burst of revenge by the second brave.

He realized then that he had inadvertently disobeyed orders to let nothing slow his ride for help, and he was struck by fear of what this could cost his comrades fighting for survival back there at the butte.

He managed to catch his mount, which had wandered only to a patch of bunch grass. He started off at a gallop, then abruptly halted to return and retrieve the body of the child.

He slung the small corpse over the mount's withers, but this was too much for the horse. It went wild at the burden's touch, tossing it free. In the end, Craig was forced to leave the body where it lay.

Desperate now to make up for time lost, he pushed the mount all out, and arrived with it wind-broke at the post, where he made his report to Captain Falk.

Falk's first question dismayed him. "How long ago did you leave your comrades under fire?"

Falk's voice was hard.

"Possibly three hours, sir."

"Three hours to ride from Skull Butte?"

Quickly, Craig tried to explain.

Falk stared at him.

"I tried to save the child, sir," Craig ended lamely.

"At least an hour lost," Falk said coldly. "Does it occur to you that quite likely the detail has been massacred because of your damned stupid delay?"

"It has occurred to me, sir. I can only say, I could not let the child be killed by the Apaches."

"The child ended up dead anyway," Falk said. "So you accomplished nothing."

Craig was silent.

"Answer me when I address you!"

"Yes, sir," Craig said.

Falk shouted for his orderly.

The orderly appeared at his door.

"This man goes into the guardhouse," Falk said. "And have First Sergeant Madden report to me at once."

When Madden arrived Falk gave him urgent orders. "Take twenty men, combat ready, and ride for Skull Butte. Lieutenant Arnett is, or was, under attack by a superior force of Apaches near there."

"Yes, sir," Madden said.

"I want you on your way immediately. The patrol's survival depends on you. It may already be too late, due to Private Craig's disregard for orders."

"Yes, sir," Madden said. "But, begging your pardon, sir, might I ask the status of Private Craig?"

"He's under arrest and confined to the guardhouse."

First Sergeant Madden was not one to antagonize an officer, but though he was only ten years older than Craig, he had taken a fatherly interest in the young trooper. This was unusual for him, but he sensed Craig had natural talents as a fighting man.

So he allowed himself to risk censure and said, "I've heard what happened, sir. At least in part. And it seems that Craig acted with good intentions, sir."

"Good intentions do not a successful army make," Falk said. "Strictly obeying orders does. Private Craig failed to do so, and I intend to see he is punished for his failure." He paused. "Do I make myself clear, Sergeant?"

Madden was no fool and knew when to defer to a superior. "Yes, sir," he said. "Completely, sir." He saluted and left, showing none of his resentment that young Craig had been put under arrest.

And not showing, either, any of the other resentment that had been growing on him after years of taking the dictates of officers whom he had come to regard, for the most part, as lesser men than he.

He should be wearing those captain's bars himself. It was only lack of education that kept him back, not lack of brains. For some time now he had been dissatisfied with what he was, feeling a drive to break out of the mold in which a poor background had cast him.

He knew he would never reach higher rank. He could command men well, but he could never look forward to more than a noncom's monthly pay. Recently the thought had come to him that he might use his abilities to his own advantage, rather than the army's. That's when he began forming his plan.

A plan that would free him from the domination of lesser men, give him the pay he deserved and the leisure to enjoy it.

He was a little surprised that what he proposed to do did not repulse him—after all, he had always performed his duties and followed orders conscientiously. Now he was planning to desert, and the idea did not trouble his conscience in the least.

Madden had grown up poor in Boston, and after a few years of trying unsuccessfully to prosper in civilian life he had enlisted. Through hard work and dedication he had reached his first sergeant rank. It was an accomplishment, but it wasn't enough to satisfy him.

By God, he wanted to get rich, that's what he wanted!

And he thought he knew the way to do it.

Even so, he might have continued as he had done all these years if Captain Falk had not arrived at Fort Maxon to take command.

Madden had usually kept a certain rapport with his men, even though he enforced compliance with his orders: he agreed with Falk that discipline must be maintained. The difference between them was one of attitude.

Falk held that harsh retribution should be inflicted for even the slightest of infractions, as the garrison at Maxon soon discovered. To Madden, this amounted to abuse of authority.

Madden himself had tested tyranny and found it wanting when he first received his sergeant's stripes nearly a dozen years before. Now, even though he had a hard core of several recruits under him who he knew had shady backgrounds, he kept them under control through his force of personality.

Some of these men were former hoodlums who had broken the laws of crowded cities back East, who were given a choice of either going to jail or joining the army. This was a common option currently offered by beleaguered judges. It was an option often taken by a lawbreaker, with the mental reservation that if the military life did not agree with him, he could always desert.

Madden had got to where he could sense this breed almost as they reached the post. Knowing their type, he took them at face value and managed to turn them into good fighting men, even though he recognized the latent resentment they frequently retained.

Perhaps there was something within him that they in turn recognized. A rebelliousness of his own.

Madden's dissatisfaction began to take root eight months ago, shortly after Falk's arrival to take over command from Major William Forrest. Forrest had been a well-liked officer who ran the post well enough, with a minimum of harshness. Madden had thought Forrest was perhaps even a little too lax at times.

Falk and Forrest were acquainted from lieutenant days, but there was a strain between them during their replacement meeting, as Falk let show a glimpse of his displeasure at what he saw as laxness, and Forrest bridled under the unspoken criticism he saw in Falk's expression. Forrest had left in a few days, transferred to a post somewhere up north. And immediately the garrison was to know that life on the post was in for a radical change.

The first incident to indicate the new order involved the soldier Madden had pegged as possibly the least tractable, even under the easy command of Major Forrest. The trooper was Sam Parrett, and he was from New York City.

Parrett was close to thirty, physically and mentally tough, and had been in the army less than two years. He fairly exuded discontent without doing anything overt. Despite this, he seemed to respect Madden enough to readily submit to his orders. Early on, though, Madden had sensed that Parrett was never more than a step away from desertion.

This was a quality that Madden had recently begun to search for among his men.

On that particular day, a morning following the arrival of an escorted twice-montly supply wagon from the distant trail town of Winn's Station, Private Parrett was seen by Captain Falk staggering around outside the barracks.

It was no secret that among supplies reaching the post there was inevitably an unofficial shipment of whiskey. This was as eagerly purchased as pay would allow by officers and enlisted men alike. Fort Maxon was too small to support a licensed post trader. Major Forrest had always considered its availability a safety valve on the isolated post.

It may have been that Captain Falk likewise did, and he availed himself of the driver-offered goods in moderate amount. But the sight of a morning-drunk and slightly boisterous trooper on the loose was more than Falk would abide.

He had Parrett seized, lashed spread-eagled across the wheel of a wagon, so that the bulging hub thrust into the middle of his back, and ordered him left that way, without water, the entire day.

There was a similar case, a few weeks later. Private John Snyder was also drunk and disorderly, roaming the grounds.

Passing the headquarters structure, he caught Falk's attention by raucous singing of a paraphrase of an old barracks ditty:

> *Poor old soldier,*
> *Poor old soldier,*
> *Tied to a wheel and put through hell,*
> *Because he wouldn't soldier well.*

Falk rushed out onto the porch, saw the bottle still in Snyder's hand, and called for his orderly.

Snyder was given a pick and shovel and the job of burying the bottle—in a hole ten feet square and eight feet deep. He was two days in the Arizona sun doing it.

Over the ensuing months, other enlisted men suffered Falk's harsh treatment.

Private Richard Hoch was forced to straddle a long, four-inch-wide beam, with the ground beyond the reach of his feet. He endured this punishment for half a day—and afterward sweated in fear that his sexual functions might be permanently impaired.

His offense was that, in a moment of rage, he had thrown his carbine onto his bunk just as Falk, accompanied by Madden, entered the barracks on a surprise inspection.

Private Ralph Hiller was "put on the chimes": A barrel was set upright and its top knocked out. Hiller was made to stand on the edges of the barrel rim for half a day.

This was for a violation of guard regulations: Falk, on one of his night prowls, had caught Hiller sitting instead of standing while on duty.

Private Robert Bentley failed to salute Lieutenant Arnett, an act of omission witnessed by Falk from his office window.

For this infraction, Falk had a heavy stick laid across Bentley's shoulders behind his neck, his arms extended to either side and lashed to the stick. Bentley was kept marching in front of headquarters, trussed this way, for a period of eight hours.

And then there was, most recently, Private Edward Slack, who had been overheard by the ubiquitous Falk to curse the army and all its "goddam" officers.

Slack was strung up by the thumbs to an overhead beam, arms stretched fully, and left standing until after several hours he collapsed.

Had not Madden been keeping a clandestine watch on him and rushed to cut him down, risking censure from Falk, Slack's thumbs would have been torn from his hands.

All this sadistic punishment, by order of the new post commander, was watched with conflicting feelings by First Sergeant Madden.

On the one hand he was angered and appalled that it was inflicted upon men with whom he maintained a rapport.

But on the other, he realized it was arousing their rebellious natures to a point that they would be ready and anxious to support his plan. All it would take was one final detestable and unreasonable action by Falk.

It wasn't that the punishments ordered by Captain Falk were unknown to the army. It was the readiness with which they were applied and the evident enjoyment of their application by Falk that had brought the misfit recruits among Madden's men to the temper he had been waiting for.

CHAPTER 2

MADDEN'S reinforcements rode fast to rescue Lieutenant Arnett's patrol and within two hours were in sight of Skull Butte, which to Madden's eyes was misnamed, having no resemblance to a skull.

As they neared, they heard no sound of firing. Heavy creosote bush and sage hid the lower reaches of the butte, and their anxiety grew as they approached it. Then they saw a few troopers moving about in a jumble of fallen rocks that footed a talus.

There was no sign of Apaches.

They rode in to find Lieutenant Arnett and others tending to seven wounded out of sixteen men, and three dead.

Arnett's first words were, "It took you a hell of a long time to get here, Sergeant."

"Sorry, sir," Madden said. "There was a delay in getting your request for help to us."

"Delay, Sergeant?" The lieutenant frowned. "I sent Trooper Craig because I thought he would get through if anybody could."

"Yes, sir," Madden said. "But he ran into problems, sir."

"What problems?"

Madden sought to postpone the answer. "A bit of a long story, sir. Might I ask what happened to the Apaches?"

"We held them off long enough that they tired of suffering their own casualties. They rode off, taking their dead and wounded with them. Not an unheard of thing for Indians, as you know."

"Yes, sir," Madden said.

"Sergeant, I asked you a question. Answer it."

16

"About Craig, sir? He was wounded himself, sir. Knocked unconscious by a bullet that glanced his head."

"He did recover, then? Must have reached the post."

"Yes, sir. But he was out for an hour or more, we figure."

"What shape is he in?"

"Physically, well enough. The surgeon patched him up."

"What do you mean *physically*?"

"Captain Falk has placed him under arrest, sir."

"Under arrest?" Lieutenant Arnett gave him a close look.

"I said it was a long story, sir."

"Yes," Arnett said. "Apparently so. Well, we can discuss it on the way back." He paused. "As you can see, we have wounded men. Three may be able to ride. We have lost five horses, so there will have to be some double riding. Plus we'll need three mounts to carry our dead."

"Yes, sir."

Madden had been glancing about at the wounded and the dead as Arnett was speaking. Now he said, "Might I ask, sir, how many casualties occurred after you sent Craig off?"

Again, Arnett scrutinized his face. "An odd question to ask, Sergeant. But it was three of the wounded."

"And of the dead, sir?"

"The dead were lost when we were first attacked—when the Apaches swarmed out from behind the butte and surprised us. Had they caught us sooner, before we neared these rocks, they'd have annihilated us. Some of Ochocama's renegade Tontos, I believe." Arnett paused. "Again, I find your question peculiar, Sergeant."

"I think it will be clearer, sir, when I can tell you more about Craig."

"All right," Arnett said. "Get your men helping us to move out."

"Yes, sir," Madden said.

Among the men who had fought off the Apache attack at the butte there was some difference of position regarding whether Private Craig should have stopped to help the boy. The division of opinion was not entirely between those who had suffered wounds and those who had not. What was noticeable was that none of those who seconded Falk's stance that an order was an order had, as yet, been direct recipients of Falk's iron-handed discipline.

But even some of these had a change of heart when they discovered Falk had requested that Craig be brought before a general court-martial.

Word had soon got out through the company clerk of Falk's communique to Department Headquarters: "Private Craig was given an order by his troop commander," Falk had written,

> *an order upon which depended the survival of his unit.*
>
> *Private Craig then foolishly allowed himself to be distracted as he rode for reinforcements. This caused a crucial delay that resulted in additional wounded, and might have caused annihilation of his comrades, had not the Apaches, for reasons of their own, tired of the attack and inexplicably ridden away.*
>
> *In the interests of a strong post discipline that I ever strive to maintain, I feel an example should be made in this case, and that even a death sentence would not be too severe.*

When Lieutenant Arnett, who had issued Craig the orders, heard of Falk's action, he risked the post commander's wrath by coming to Craig's defense. "But, sir, Private Craig was rendered unconscious when he stopped to protect a child."

"He had his orders," Falk said. "Which was the more important, to get help to save his comrades, or to make a vain attempt to save the offspring of a pair of fools who should not have been traveling alone in that area in the first place?"

"But, sir, the child!"

Falk's face hardened and he said tightly, "My position

stands. And you may pass it on to the troops as a guideline to the behavior I expect should any of them ever be confronted by the choice that faced Private Craig."

When Arnett remained silent, Falk went on, "Lieutenant, I have heard that I am sometimes described as a martinet. Well, let me say that I do not find that term offensive. Rather, I revel in it. A military unit, I believe, is only as good as its discipline, and I intend to instill discipline into any command I have. In the months that I have been here at Maxon, I trust you have observed as much."

"Yes, sir," Lieutenant Arnett said. "That I have, sir."

For the first time, Falk showed a faint grin. "Carry on, then, Lieutenant."

Arnett left Falk's office with a single thought: *The man is mad.*

But if the man wants me to pass along his warning to the troop, I will gladly do so. For their own protection.

He immediately sent for First Sergeant Madden.

Madden appeared at Arnett's bachelor quarters, saluted, and said, "You sent for me, sir?"

"I did," the lieutenant said. He strove to keep anger from his words as he passed on the information given him by Falk.

When he finished, he waited for a reaction from Madden.

"Yes, sir," Madden said.

"My God, Sergeant! Is that all you have to say?"

"Yes, sir."

Arnett studied him. "Well, I suppose so. How long have you been in the service, Sergeant?"

"Twelve years, sir."

"Ever tire of it?"

The first sergeant had a hard, unsmiling face, but now it cracked slightly. "There are times, sir."

The lieutenant did not speak at once, then he said, "Yes, I imagine so. Well, you may feel free to tell the troops what I have just revealed to you. As a matter of fact, Captain Falk wants it to be known."

"Yes, sir," Sergeant Madden said. "I can believe that, sir."

And so the men had waited, after Craig had been sent under guard to department headquarters in Prescott for his trial. Weeks later he had been returned to Maxon with the special order that he be drummed out of the service and banished from the post.

It was Madden, the most trusted by Falk of the enlisted men, who was given the duty of escorting Craig to the nearest stage stop, Winn's Station, sixty miles away, where Craig was to be given sufficient fare to take him out of the territory.

Before leaving Craig at Winn's Station, Madden bought him a drink in a sleazy, hog-ranch tavern adjacent to the stage stop.

Riding back to the post, Madden reviewed mentally the so-called dereliction-of-duty charge brought against Craig by Falk. It was unjust.

As charged, Private Raymond Craig had failed to expeditiously carry Arnett's plea for reinforcements, but he was not a deserter, not intentionally. He had made a quick decision costly to himself, and possibly others, by stopping to try to rescue the child.

One thing was sure, Madden thought—the young trooper had guts.

Too bad about Craig. But Falk's treatment of Craig would enable Madden to put into action the plan he had been contemplating; it had aroused increased resentment among the men Madden had been watching.

Men who could play a big part in his future goals.

When Madden reported back to Arnett he began to put his plan into action by lying about having seen sign of a recent small encampment of Apaches along his way.

"Might I take a squad on a scout detail in that area, sir?"

Lieutenant Arnett sent him to Captain Falk, where he repeated his request.

To this, Falk was agreeable. "I'll have Lieutenant Arnett detail six men for you."

"Might I pick the men, sir?"

Falk gave him a curious look. "Why?"

"No particular reason, sir. It's just that I have a few in mind I believe could use the experience."

"Very well, Sergeant," Falk said. "Tell Lieutenant Arnett I wish to see him."

"Yes, sir. Thank you, sir." Madden saluted and took his leave.

Two days later he rode again out of Fort Maxon, heading north, leading a detail of six handpicked men, each armed and rationed for a week's detached duty, including grain for the horses.

Privates Parrett, Snyder, Hoch, Hiller, Bentley, and Slack. To a man, all had suffered at the hands of Captain Falk. And to a man, they'd had enough when they saw the branding of Raymond Craig.

As they approached Winn's Station, their glances targeted on the hog-ranch tavern.

"How about a drink, Sarge?" asked Hiller, riding beside Madden.

Without a word, Madden turned toward the hitchrack.

As they reached it, they could see in the shade of the crude portico a disheveled figure sprawled against the wall.

"Crissakes, Sarge!" Hiller said. "Ain't that Private Craig sitting there? It looks like he tied one on."

"Must have blown his fare money," Madden said, looking thoughtful.

"What's he going to do now?" Hiller said. "He ain't in the army no more."

"That's right," Madden said. "And neither are you, unless you want to be."

"What do you mean?"

Madden did not answer at once. Then he said, "You've had desertion on your mind for a long time, Hiller."

Hiller started as if to bluster, then abruptly stopped and said, "How'd you know?"

"I know. Just like I know about the rest of this detail."

"It was what that sonofabitching captain done to Craig that done it," Hiller said.

"I know that too," Madden said.

Parrett spoke up from behind. "Hey, Sarge, that there is Ray Craig!"

There was some surprised muttering from the rest.

"Damn if it ain't!"

"What's he doing here?"

"Staying drunk, looks like," Slack said.

"I guess it's time to tell the rest," Madden said to Hiller.

"You're going to surprise hell out of them, Sarge."

Madden turned his horse to face them and, in a voice loud enough for all to hear, called for their attention.

"Men," he said, "I know that all of you have had a bellyful of sweating out an enlistment under a horse's ass of a post commander." He paused, seeing their eyes hard and curious upon him. "As of now, though, you are free of him, free to go your own way, for that's my own intention."

The troopers sat their saddles in shock, silent and unmoving.

He gave them time to speak, and when none did, he went on, "Those of you who want to go with me can consider yourselves still on D Troop's roster. But the D won't be an army designation any longer. The D will stand for deserters."

Their shock still held, and he said, "The choice is yours."

It was Hiller who spoke first. "Where you heading, Sarge?"

"Nevada," Madden said.

"Why Nevada?"

"Because there's too much army here. On account of the Apache troubles. Up Nevada way, now, the Injun trouble isn't fierce like it is down here. No damned Apaches. No Commanches like there is back in Texas, either.

"So the army is scattered thin up there. Too thin to be concerned with a handful of soldiers gone over the hill, even if word got to them about us, which ain't likely to happen."

Private Hoch said, "They got any Injuns at all up there?"

"Just Diggers, which is what they call the Paiutes. And some Western Shoshones, who are cousin to the Paiutes. All of them damned tame compared to the Apaches we've been fighting."

"That part sounds good," Private Slack said. "But what're we going to do up there?"

"Mining is the big thing in Nevada."

"Hell, Sarge, I'd never make a miner. I couldn't stand being underground."

"The part of the mining business I got in mind," Madden said, "is all above ground. Suitable work for men like us who can ride and shoot."

Hiller was about to ask him to explain what he meant, but the slumbering man on the porch suddenly awoke, groaned, crawled on his hands and knees to the edge, and vomited violently.

The hog-ranch proprietor stepped out of the open doorway, a slob of a man in dirty hickory trousers and a soiled red undershirt. He glared at Madden and called, "Listen, you. Get this bum out of here. The bastard had the d.t.'s this morning till I give him some more to drink free."

"I should've guessed you were the one got all his money," Madden said. "He went through hell a few days back, Mac. Like I told you."

"And I been through hell putting up with him," Mac said. "I seen plenty of men on a drunk before, but this one takes the contest."

Madden swung down from his saddle. "You men go on in. Mac, give them one drink, and one only, on me."

"You better get in here to pay for them," Mac said.

"Soon as I talk to Craig here," Madden said, stopping beside his now prone figure.

The others paused as they passed, to stare down at Craig; some were silent, a couple laughed. Hoch swore bitterly and said, "The poor son of a bitch! I never knew him to get drunk before. That goddam Falk brought him to this."

Ex–First Sergeant Madden looked up when he heard that. "That goddam Falk brought us all to this," he said.

The others went inside then, and Madden bent down and lifted Craig up to a sitting posture against the wall.

"Raymond, you able to understand what I'm saying?"

Craig tried to focus his eyes, but failed.

"Christ!" Madden said. "That homemade likker of Mac's must be worse poison than I thought." He paused. "Raymond, look at me!"

Craig tried again. This time he managed to find Madden with his stare. "That you, Sarge?" he muttered.

"It's me, Raymond. Me and some of your old comrades. We're going to take you with us."

"Not going anywhere," Craig mumbled. "All washed up."

"You're going with us, Ray. With your old buddies from D Troop."

"Frigging Falk drummed me out, Sarge."

"We won't be taking orders from him no more, Ray."

"Who's command now?"

"Me, Ray. Old Sarge Madden. I'm in charge from here on in."

"What you mean, Sarge?"

"I'll tell you about it when you're sober, Ray."

Craig began to ramble. "I never meant to let the men down, you know that, Sarge. But I had to help that little kid. They was about to smash his head against a wagon wheel. I killed both those Apaches, but they somehow killed the boy. While they was dying, I guess. That's what happened. You know that, Sarge. Why couldn't Captain Falk understand?"

"Because he's a twenty-carat horse's ass," Madden said.

"That's why. And that's why we all left his command, Raymond. On account of what he did to you. You understand what I'm saying? On account of you, Ray. So you get sober now, and you come with us."

"Where?"

"Nevada," Madden said. "Raymond, I got big plans for us up in Nevada."

"Never been to Nevada," Craig said, his voice fading from his mumbling efforts.

"You'll like what we're going to do up there, Raymond," Madden said.

But ex–Private Craig had fallen asleep again.

Inside the saloon, the troopers had been served the specified single drink by the bar owner, downed it, and now waited for Madden to join them.

They sat silently. They did not trust the hog-ranch proprietor.

Neither, apparently, did he them. When Hiller called for another round of drinks on Madden, Mac shook his head.

"Not 'less I hear it from the Sarge hisself, soldier."

"You don't trust us to pay?" Hiller said truculently.

"On your private's pay of thirteen dollars a month, I don't," Mac said.

"Fine way to treat us that risks our life to protect you from them Apache devils," Hiller said.

"I won't argue that, soldier. But that's the way it is."

"Was we rich," Hiller said, "you'd treat us different."

"That I would, soldier. That I damn sure would," the bar man said. "Don't you know yet that it's money makes the world go round?"

"Reckon I'm learning," Hiller said. He looked over as Madden came in the door.

Madden had appraised them well. To a man, they chose to throw in with him. All except Craig, who had still not recovered enough to make a choice. Madden took him along for two reasons: the hog-ranch owner refused to let him stay, and Madden believed Craig could be useful. So Madden bought him a horse and saddle cheap from a nervous stage-stock tender who knew it was stolen.

They were across the Colorado River and into Nevada before Raymond Craig came back to the real world. Even then he was too sick to make any decisions about what he wanted. His self-worth had been destroyed by what had happened to him. And yet he knew he had done what he had to in trying to save the child.

Madden rode over to him and, aware of his suffering, gave him practical advice. "There's only one way to cure what's bothering you, Ray. Get mad at what they did to you. Rebel. You'll feel better then."

Madden hoped his advice would be taken. He knew Raymond had guts. The troop had shown uncommon bravery in battles against the Apaches. And Madden knew that to use Craig's courage, and that of the rest of them, he had to keep alive their feeling of rebellion.

CHAPTER 3

CRAIG was well now. He was also beginning to have some doubts. Doubts he felt an urge to express to Madden.

But each time he glanced at that hard-tempered face his nerve failed him. He had a dim recollection of the Sarge talking to him in a chummy tone back there at the hog ranch. But now he saw no chumminess in the ex–noncom's expression at all.

All of them except himself were still in cavalry uniform. He was wearing the remnants left him by Lieutenant Arnett.

Their horses carried the USA brand on their haunches, and the riders sat the split McClellan saddles.

His own mount was stock-saddled and carried an Aztec Cattle Company brand.

At length Craig got up nerve enough to remark on this.

"Sarge, it ain't too safe me sitting this horse. That brand is known over half of Arizona maybe."

"Stop worrying, Craig. We're in Nevada now."

"Even so."

"I said to stop worrying. And that's an order."

"I thought we were all out of the army now," Craig said.

"I'm still giving the orders. And I'll keep on giving them," Madden said. "You understand what I'm saying, Craig?"

"You figure to keep us all together, is that it?"

"Exactly. It won't be any different. Except there'll be no frigging officers telling us what to do. No more of that goddam Captain Falk getting his kicks out of branding good soldiers like yourself."

"I kind of liked Lieutenant Arnett," Craig said.

"He wasn't a bad sort, as officers go," Madden said. "But

27

he had to follow Falk's orders, like everybody else." He paused. "We're all shed of that life, Craig. From now on, we're on our own."

"What've you got in mind, Sarge?"

"What I got in mind is to get rich," Madden said. "And with all that gold and silver they been digging out of the ground in Nevada, I figure that's the place to do it."

"Is it that easy?"

"I aim to make it easy."

"None of us knows about mining," Craig said.

"I figure all of us can learn real quick."

"It might beat soldiering at that."

"You can bet on it," Madden said.

"What's the name of the town we're heading for?" Craig asked after a while.

"Pioche," Madden replied. He had heard of Pioche,[1] but only that it was currently one of the richest of Nevada's many mining camps. He chose it because Pioche lay in the southeast part of Nevada, a likely first stop to get acquainted with the new environment in which he planned his future operations.

"That an Injun name?" Craig asked.

"Way I heard, it's named after a Frenchman banker from San Francisco who got some of the first holdings."

"Sounds Injun, Sarge."

"Well, it ain't."

"I don't rightly know what you expect us to do there," Craig said.

"You don't need to know," Madden said. "I'll find us something."

As they approached the town they heard intermittent gunfire. Madden listened, and told his men, "Sounds like a skirmish."

---

[1]Pioche is pronounced *Pee-oćh.*

Hiller agreed. "That it does, Sarge. That ain't just no two-man gun duel."

"Might be an Injun attack," Craig said.

"Not likely," Madden said. "What I heard, there hasn't been a real battle with the Paiutes for ten, twelve years, and that was way over west at a place called Pyramid Lake. I recall reading about it in a newspaper."

"What else could it be?" Craig said.

"We'll soon be finding out," Madden said.

The town was built without much planning. A crooked main street followed the twists and turns of a shallow canyon that flanked a range of mountains to the west. Branch roads ran to surrounding hills that were covered with miner's shacks. Mine tailings dotted the mountain sides as the riders got their first glimpse of it.

Along the twisting main street was the usual assortment of board-front businesses. There was a livery stable near where they entered the town.

Madden halted his men in front of it as the hostler appeared, staring. He asked, "This Pioche?"

"This is it," the hostler said.

Madden could see the man staring at their uniforms.

"Just ride in from Fort Halleck?" the hostler asked.

Fort Halleck was near two hundred miles north, Madden was thinking. Up near the railroad. He said, "You expecting cavalry?"

"Expecting? No."

At that moment a fusillade sounded again. The deserters glanced up to the mountain flank. There was a float of gunsmoke dissipating in the air above.

"Like I said," the hostler said. "Not expecting, but might be we could use some."

"Sounds so," Madden said.

The hostler's stare moved to Craig, sitting the stock saddle, his uniform stripped of insignia and buttons.

"Looks like you might have caught yourself a deserter, Sergeant," the hostler said.

"Not a deserter. Was carrying dispatch," Madden said. "We come upon him while a couple of Injuns that waylaid him was having their fun. Cut off his buttons and such. Reckon we got there at the right time. Be something more important to a man they were fixing to cut off next."

"Sons of bitches," the hostler said. "Strange, though. We ain't had no Injun trouble hereabouts lately."

"Goes that way, sometimes," Madden said. "What's all that shooting up there?"

"Claim war."

"Claim war?"

The hostler gave him a close look. "I guess you ain't heard much about Pioche here. Fighting's been going on ever since the first claim was filed. Overlapping claims and such. Whenever some of those claims turn out rich, the owners get to fighting over encroachments."

"I thought they settled things like that in the courts," Madden said.

"The courts are slow, and the mine companies get impatient—then the shooting starts. Them's hired guns you hear going off up there on the mountain."

"Hired guns?"

"Sure. Just like range wars in the cattle country, we got mine wars here. A man handy with a gun can likely find a job with one bunch or the other."

"Is that a fact?" Madden said.

"That's why I thought maybe the army heard about it and sent you in."

"Well," Madden said, "now that we're here, might be we'll look into it."

"There'd be some citizens would appreciate that. Most of us is peace-loving folks."

"Never know it by the sound," Madden said.

"Like I said, that's the hard cases going at it up there."

"Sounds like they're earning their money. Who's paying those we hear burning gunpowder?"

"Worthington and Crowell on one side, and the Jutland brothers on the other."

"What's the fight about?"

"It started when the Jutland boys bought a claim on the upper side of the Worthington and Crowell, and bought permission to tunnel from the Crowell to reach their own. But whilst they was driving a shaft they hit a bonanza vein in the Crowell property."

"I reckon that could complicate things," Madden said.

"Well, not at first it didn't. The Jutland boys made a deal for a thirty-day lease to work the vein."

"The Crowell owners agreed?"

"For a price, sure. They figured thirty days would just about expose the vein for easier working, plus they'd get the lease money."

"So?"

"So, when the thirty days was up, the Jutland boys refused to pull off their crew. They hired a small army of gunhands, fortified the mouth of the mine. The Crowell owners went to the sheriff, but he refused to interfere because he had already been bought off by the Jutlands.

"So they hired their own gunhands, and for a week now the two sides have been mixing it up." The hostler paused. "That's why I figured maybe you boys had rid in."

"We been on a patrol down south a ways," Madden said. "But like I told you, being we're here, we'll look into it. Sounds odd though that the sheriff could be bought by one side or the other."

The hostler gave him a studying look, then said, "I guess you army fellers don't know how it is in a place like this. Being sheriff pays off better than most of the claims."

"Now that's an interesting fact to know," Madden said. He got directions to where the Worthington & Crowell headquarters was, and led the men up the winding street.

"What you got in mind, Sarge?" Hiller asked as they approached the mining company office.

Madden did not answer. He dismounted in front of the wooden structure.

"You men wait here," he said.

Inside the office, a man in khaki pants and shirt and miner's boots stood at a window, staring out at the ex-troopers. He appeared to be in his forties, and despite his clothes he had an office look about him.

No pick and shovel there, Madden was thinking.

The man turned to face him, and his eyes went to Madden's chevrons. He appeared perplexed. He said, "Yes, Sergeant?"

"Ex-Sergeant," Madden said. "Me and my men just been discharged. Haven't got around to buying new clothes."

The man's expression changed from perplexed to poker.

"I'm John Crowell," he said. "What can I do for you?"

"Heard you were having some trouble at your diggings."

"It's no secret."

"Might be we could help you out."

"In what way?"

"I noticed you studying my men out there. Good fighting men, Mr. Crowell. Been fighting Apaches. You must have seen they still carry their carbines and side arms."

"A little unusual for discharged men, I'd think."

Madden said nothing.

"I'm not a man to pry into another's business," Crowell said. "What's your proposition, Sergeant?"

"What exactly is your problem? What I heard is you got some armed intruders forted up inside your mine."

"Word is," Crowell said, "they found a rich vein of high-grade gold down there after leasing the rights to tunnel to the Jutland claim."

"Gold?" Madden said. "I thought this was silver country."

"It is. Silver is why we're here. But gold is always possible.

And what we hear, when they found the vein, they smuggled in enough supplies to last them another two weeks."

"What are you doing about it?"

"Nothing. The Jutland boys have got the local law on their side, and that discourages the free-lance hired guns from going against them."

Madden nodded. "For a price, we'd get rid of them for you."

Crowell went back to the window and looked out at the mounted riders. Then he turned back to Madden and said, "A hundred dollars per man, yourself included, if you can clear those highgraders and the gunhands protecting them out of there."

"We've had a long ride here from Arizona way," Madden said, "and we're out of rations. Our horses need care. We've got to have some money up front. Say half of it. The rest when we clean them out."

"I'd be risking four hundred on a bunch of strangers. Only thing I know about you is the uniform you wear." He paused again. "And I'm not too sure about that."

"And how much will you lose on the takeout of those highgraders in there?" Madden said. "Every day they're filling their pockets with a hell of a lot more than I ask. You say they've got gunhands to protect them. When they decide to come out, they'll come out shooting." Madden paused. "And when they come out loaded, we won't be here to help you. You'd best let us take care of it now."

Crowell was silent for a long moment. Then he said, "All right. But I never knew the army to discharge a whole squad at the same time before. Especially good fighting men. Against Apaches, you say?"

"That's right."

"Don't tell me the Apaches are beaten."

"The army moves in strange ways sometimes," Madden said, giving him a steady stare.

Crowell stared back, then abruptly nodded. "Well, I

wouldn't argue that. None of my business, anyway. Get the job done and you'll get paid."

"And the subsistence money?"

There was a heavy safe in the corner of the office, but Crowell didn't go to it. Instead, he took out a wallet and fingered some large-denomination currency from it. He held it out.

Madden stuffed it into a pocket.

"You didn't count it," Crowell said.

"No need, is there? Not if you want the job done."

Crowell nodded. "When do you start earning it?"

"Tomorrow," Madden said. "That all right with you?"

"It'll do," Crowell said.

They put up their horses at the livery, ate voraciously at the Highland Restaurant, then bivouacked on a vacant spot of reasonably level ground not far from a saloon where Madden had taken them for a brief period of refreshments.

It was Hiller, often inquisitive, who pressed Madden for the details of his discussion with Crowell. When Madden sketched in the proposition that had gained them the subsistence money, Hiller and the others did not look happy about it.

"Dammit, Sarge, we could get ourself killed first off," Hiller said, "before we even start to get rich like you told us."

"Everything has its risks," Madden said. "But I'm thinking on a plan to lower them."

"I hope it's a good one," Slack said.

There were assenting grunts from the others.

"None of us boys is wanting to get our ass shot off," Hoch offered.

"You're soldiers, aren't you?"

"We *was*," Parrett said.

"Sure you were," Madden said. "And good ones too, as far as fighting goes. And for thirteen dollars a month." He paused. "Just keep in mind that your pay will be considerable more from now on."

"Even so," Bentley said.

"Bentley's right," Snyder said, "Fighting Apaches is one thing—if you start getting the best of them, they can be driv' off. But white men don't give up so easy."

"I'm thinking on a way to make them," Madden said.

"Tell us how."

"I haven't got it all thought out yet," Madden said. "But I haven't let you down yet, have I?"

There was a short silence, until Raymond Craig said, "Not unless this whole scheme of deserting to get rich is wrong."

"You forgetting you been branded?"

Craig hesitated. Then he said, "No. I reckon I ain't likely to ever forget that."

"Well, then."

Craig was silent.

So were the rest of them. Military habit still had its grip. You just didn't argue with a first sergeant.

Their new relationship would take some getting used to.

Madden later returned alone to the saloon and had a talk with the owner.

The saloon keeper, Cain, was skeptical at first. "You want two cases of whiskey sent into a mine?" he said. "Beats anything I ever heard of."

"I'm doing a chore for the Jutland brothers. I understand they've got a lease to work the Crowell claim. This is a gift of appreciation to the men in their hire."

Cain gave him a close look. "There's some argument about that. About the lease, I mean."

"So I've been told. And that's the reason for the gift. Those men are living down there. The Jutlands realize they need some relaxation."

"You being an army first sergeant, it's hard to see how you fit into this."

"Just discharged," Madden said. "You might say this is my first civilian job."

"I'd be taking a chance on ruffling Crowell's feathers," Cain said. "But for a double price on the whiskey, I'll see it's sneaked into the Jutland crew." He paused. "Mostly because I ain't a particular friend of Crowell's. Never cared for his high-handed manner."

Madden withdrew part of the money Crowell had advanced him.

Cain's expression turned more congenial. He said, "When do you want it delivered?"

"Now. It's Saturday afternoon. And what better night for those poor miners down there to celebrate?"

"I'll see it's done," Cain said. "But all them boys in there ain't miners, you know. There's some hired guns fortified at the shaft mouth, way I heard it."

"They deserve some relaxation, too," Madden said.

"I reckon being a first sergeant has given you a understanding of men," Cain said.

"I hope so," Madden said.

Madden had staked out his men near enough to observe the delivery of the whiskey by a couple of Cain's bartenders. And close enough to listen for the sound of revelry if it came.

A couple of hours went by, and then the noise of off-key singing and raucous shouting began to emanate from behind the fortification at the entrance of the sloping shaft.

"All right," Madden said. "Those boys are drunker than hoot owls, by what I hear."

"What we going to do, Sarge?" Hiller asked.

"Attack," Madden said. "We're going in over those breastworks. Shooting."

Slack said, "Them boys may not be likkered up as they sound."

"I'm thinking they are," Madden said.

Raymond Craig said, "I don't know, Sarge. I don't like this . . ."

"It's an order, Craig. If you're going to ride with us, you'll take orders from me!"

They had ridden up to the mine, and their horses were tethered in the brush nearby, carbines in the saddle boots. But each man wore an army Colt .44 and carried two extra loaded cylinders.

Crowell, looking from his mine office window, saw them readying for action and came out now to watch.

Madden said, "Side arms only. There won't be room in there for using carbines. Drunk as they are, they'll maybe give up without a fight." He gave Craig a studying look. "You going to be one of us, or not? If not, you're on your own from here on out. Make up your mind. Now."

Craig did not answer at once. Then he said, "I guess I got to be with you. I guess I owe you that much."

"That you do, Raymond. And you won't regret it."

"I hope not," Craig said.

Madden split them. "Spread out. Close in on each side of the tunnel. When I signal, we all go in, firing."

He kept Craig in his segment of the squad, swinging out wide, them coming in from the right flank.

Across the approach Hiller led the others, flanking left.

As they closed in, Madden led a concerted charge for the low fortification, leaping the piled boulders of the breastwork.

The hired guns were sprawled about in various stages of inebriation, rifles scattered here and there. But each wore a holstered revolver. There were only six men, not the dozen that Cain had estimated. But drunk or not, they grabbed for their weapons, even as the troopers fired.

Two of them went down before they triggered a response. In the immediate exchange of the others, Craig was the only trooper hit. He took a bullet in his left upper arm. To his own surprise, the wound turned him berserk. With two fast

shots, he personally downed another pair of gunmen. He
had never before been shot except for the scalp wound, and
the wildness of his response was born of his instinct to
survive.

The remaining two hired guns threw up their hands,
dropping their weapons.

Madden's eyes swept the downed four. None of them
moved. Dead, he thought. Damn good shooting by his troopers. Now he was surer than ever that they had a profitable
future ahead of them.

"Goddam!" one of the surviving defenders said. "I didn't
figure they'd send the army to blast us out of here."

"Your mistake then, wasn't it?" Madden said.

At that moment the first of the miners came staggering
into the adit from below. "What the hell's going on?" he said,
staring from the downed and captured hired guns to the
uniformed attackers.

"They done sent the United States Army against us," the
hired gun said.

Behind the first miner crowded others. Most of them
showed the apathy of their debauch. But a few, a little more
sober than the rest, had comments of their own to make.

"Looks like Crowell has got more clout than we figured,
getting the army to side him," one of them said.

Another stared at the yellow piping on Madden's trousers.
"First time I ever heard of them making a cavalry charge into
a mine, by God!"

"What you going to do with us?" one of the hired guns
said.

"We've got orders to bring you out," Madden said. "Any
more of you *pistoleros* down below, you better come peaceful."
He nodded to the four lying dead.

"Was only us six," the hired gun said. "What about them
miners?"

Madden gave the leading miners a hard stare. "We got
orders that they come out, too." Then he addressed them.

"You hear? You're all of you through working this mine. You want to argue the point, now is the time."

The miner spokesman glanced at the dead gunmen. "No argument, soldier. No argument at all. Sure as hell, not against the United States Army!"

Still guarded by the troopers, the miners and surviving gunmen were shaken down for any high-grade gold they might have hidden on their persons, then told to get out of town, or else.

"Or else what?" one of them wanted to know.

"You want to walk the two hundred miles to Fort Halleck?" Madden said. "Because that's where I'm taking you unless you light out on your own."

"Hell of a poor choice," the man said.

"It's the only one you'll get," Madden said.

Crowell, appearing pleased, stood looking on. "You better listen to what he's saying," he said.

"We're listening," the spokesman said. "But it's a hell of a way for the cavalry to treat us honest citizens."

"Be glad you aren't Injuns," Madden said.

"That we are," the man said.

After the flesh wound in Craig's arm was dressed by a doctor summoned by Crowell, he rested in the area they had selected for bivouac. It wasn't a serious wound, but it throbbed painfully enough to remind him of that desperate moment during the attack when he had shot to death the two men. There had been no hesitation there.

Now, reflecting on his action, his adrenaline no longer high, he was bothered by what he had done. He regretted the killings, even though he knew it had been his own life or theirs.

He had been in combat before, under Madden, and at the butte under Lieutenant Arnett. But those times he had been fighting at carbine range, not face to face where you could intimately view the transformation by your own hand of a fellow human being into a corpse.

Madden, lounging nearby, was watching him. Now he said, "Shooting those hired guns weigh on you, Raymond?"

"Reckon it does."

"You'll get used to it."

Craig gave him a quick, startled glance. "Hell, I don't want to get used to it!"

"Well, I didn't mean it that way," Madden said. "What I meant was that if you got to kill, you get so you can accept it."

"I just hope it don't happen again," Craig said.

"Likely it will."

"Why?"

"Because that's the kind of business we'll be getting into," Madden said.

"Maybe I ain't cut out for such business."

"Let me be the judge of that."

"No," Craig said. "It'll be me that decides."

Madden was silent, then he said, "All right, Craig. All I ask is you give it a try."

CHAPTER 4

THE *Pioche Record* took notice of their first robbery with a short column that lacked details but put forth the first suspicion of who might be the perpetrators of the crime:

> *A resurgence of holdups on the stage route north to Wells may be indicated by a most recent one that occurred last Monday when a band of six or eight outlaws, faces half-covered, stopped a Concord driven by veteran driver Lucas Farnsworth and shot-gun messengered by Ike Williams, a few miles south of the Montezuma turnoff road.*
>
> *The size of the bandit gang, the yellow neckerchiefs used as masks, and the fact that they sat McClellan saddles on horses carrying U.S. brands, leads to a suspicion by both driver and guard that this is the cavalry detachment that not long ago intervened to settle the encroachment battle at the Worthington & Crowell mine.*
>
> *At that time, their first sergeant said they were a passing scout detail. Now, no longer in uniform and dressed in range rider clothing, speculation is high that they are in reality a bunch of deserters.*
>
> *Ironically, they made off with the payroll money for the miners working for Worthington & Crowell.*
>
> *An interview with John Crowell revealed his anger at the occurrence. "Sounds like the same damned bunch," he stated. "But at the time I hired them, I had no reason to disbelieve their assertion that they had been recently discharged from the army down in Arizona."*
>
> *Thus far, all that is further known is that the robber band rode off to the east toward the Utah border.*
>
> *Striking as the story is, it will be remembered that this is not the first time in recent Nevada history that soldiers gone bad have preyed on an express shipment. Less than two years ago—in*

> *November of 1870, to be exact—four deserters from Fort Halleck,*
> *two still in uniform, held up a Central Pacific train east of Wells*
> *and rode off with saddlebags filled with minted silver, packages of*
> *gold dust, and stacks of greenbacks. They were tracked down by a*
> *railroad posse in the Utah desert.*
>
> *It is to be hoped that a similar fate will soon befall this bunch,*
> *although they seem to operate with a military precision under their*
> *renegade first sergeant.*

During the robbery, excitement had taken hold of Raymond Craig to an extent that he was not disturbed that he was taking part in a crime. The job had gone smoothly. There had been no shooting—surrounded by eight armed riders who moved under orders of an authoritative leader, neither the driver nor the shotgun messenger chose to resist.

It was later, when Madden oversaw the splitting of the payroll cash among the men, that uneasiness and regret set in on Craig as he realized he was now a criminal. With the excitement gone, that fact hit him hard.

Three thousand dollars had been split among the deserters. With Madden taking a double share, the others got nearly three hundred fifty apiece.

More money than any one of them had ever had.

When Madden held Craig's share toward him, he grinned. "What do you think of that, Raymond?"

Craig did not reach for the money.

Madden thrust it against Craig's chest. "Take it!" he said.

Still, Craig did not reach.

"You hear me?" Madden said. "That's an order!"

The other troopers were staring now, their faces growing hard.

Hiller said, "If he don't want it, Sarge, I'll take it."

Nobody laughed.

"Don't you understand?" Madden said. "You're one of us now, whether that was your intention or not."

Craig was silent.

"One of us," Madden said, "and guilty as any. You better realize now who your friends are."

Craig's eyes went to the stares surrounding him. They were waiting. Waiting to see if he was friend or foe.

Reluctantly, he reached out and took his share of the payroll from Madden.

"That's better," Madden said. "You've got friends here, Raymond. Old friends. And a chance to get rich. Never forget that you don't have either anywhere else."

It was true, Craig thought. These men were more than friends. They had been his comrades-in-arms through more than one skirmish with the Apaches. And he had lived and soldiered with them through months of garrison life. No matter that now they were deserters, they had become family.

And what was he, with a D branded on each hip? He wore the mark, rightly or wrongly—a mark he would carry to his grave.

If you carry the mark, why not live the part? he thought. As his resentment against his punishment rose again, it brought a measure of relief to his conscience. He was where he was today because of that goddam post commander, Falk. He was not a man to hold a grudge, he told himself. But with Falk he made an exception. Someday, someplace, he hoped to repay the bastard in kind. There was scant chance of that, he thought.

But a man could dream, couldn't he?

After this first robbery, Madden had led them eastward across the Utah line into a haven he had picked, learning of it from conversation overheard in Pioche.

East of the border, in the northern end of the Needle mountain range, was a little valley known to early cattle rustlers as Chisco Springs. It lay fifty-five rugged miles northeast of Pioche. Nestled in the foothills was a series of springs that provided ample water for men and mounts; there was even a fair amount of graze.

Around the oasis, following the silver strikes at Pioche, Hiko, and Hamilton, had grown a small outlaw community of the loose and unruly. There was even a combination saloon and mercantile of sorts, supplied erratically from distant Milford, Utah.

It was not really a town, just a mere way station for transients on the dodge.

An ideal base for an operation, Madden thought. Although there were other road agents sojourning there, they were mostly loners, and Madden, with his disciplined troopers, figured he could handle any trouble that might arise.

As he led them into the settlement, there were a few hard-looking spectators loitering along the short dirt street who eyed them apprehensively. He smiled inwardly, aware that even no longer uniformed, his men had a military look about them. And, of course, there were still the McClellan saddles.

Let them wonder, he thought. Let them know that he and his men were a special breed. That way they would be more likely left alone.

He would, in turn, stay out of the business of the others.

A couple of weeks went by while the bunch loafed around the refuge, spending their loot in the saloon and eating well.

"Never lived so high on the hog in my life," Hiller said.

"This is just the beginning," Madden said. "I wanted you boys to enjoy a taste of the good life for a change."

"It's a change, all right," Slack said. "Beats army life by a damn sight."

Craig, who was listening, said nothing.

Madden noticed this and said, "What about you, Ray?"

"I didn't mind being in the cavalry."

"Hell," Madden said, "you're still in the cavalry. Only difference is, we're in business for ourselves."

"And the pay is a hell of a lot better," Slack said.

"I never cared about getting rich," Craig said.

"Craig," Madden said, "I'm beginning to think you're a strange one."

Craig was silent again.

Slack's eyes swung to him and remained there. A hard look came over his face. "And that's something to worry about, Sarge, way I see it."

"Raymond's all right. Just a little different, maybe," Madden said. "You're all right, aren't you, Raymond?"

"Yeah."

"Trouble is," Madden said, "you haven't been enjoying yourself like the rest of us. You don't drink hardly at all."

"That hangover I got at Winn's Station damn near killed me, Sarge. I ain't had the urge since."

"Just as well," Madden said. "One like that is enough for a lifetime."

"I wouldn't argue that none," Craig said.

Slack still stared at him, but he made no further comment. Instead, he said, "When we going into action again, Sarge?"

"Soon," Madden said. "I hear there's going to be some shipments of bullion out from the mining mills, and payroll money expressed in."

"Hell, there ought to be enough out of them mills near Pioche at Bullionville without us looking further."

"It don't pay to hit one place too often," Madden said. "It tends to get the victims real mad. Anyhow, that silver bullion is a possible, but the ingots are damn heavy to pack away on a horse. My thinking is that payroll shipments are a sight better."

"You got my agreement on that," Hiller said. "Paper currency is some lighter than them forty-pound bars of silver."

"I don't know why Craig ain't happy," Slack said. "We got plenty of money, and nobody got hurt getting it."

Craig said, "That's because there was no shooting. What happens when some shotgun messenger puts up a fight?"

"You been shot at before, ain't you?" Slack said.

"And when I was, I killed some enemy Apaches."

"So?"

"It strikes me that's some different than shooting down a shotgun rider or a stage driver doing his job."

"Why? Because his skin isn't red?"

"Because he ain't an enemy," Craig said.

Slack said, "A man shoots at me, he's made hisself my enemy, no matter what."

Madden was listening and watching. He could see what bothered Craig. He understood it, because it bothered him also. He had led a straight life before his decision to seek riches. He did not have a criminal background like some of his men. Craig and he were both exceptions.

The difference was, he was willing to accept the sacrifices of his conscience in the pursuit of his newly adopted career. Apparently, Craig was not. At least, not yet.

The next newspaper account of Madden's men appeared in far away Unionville's *The Silver State*, northwest on the Central Pacific rail line:

> *Over in the southeast part of the state, in the vicinity of Pioche, there has been another depredation on a stagecoach express ship-ment that lends further credence to the suspicion that there is extant a bandit bunch composed of cavalry deserters. This is the third known strike by this bunch, described as riding cavalry mounts and saddles. It is rumored the men address their leader as "Sarge."*
>
> *A recent traveler in town has informed us that locals in the Pioche area have taken to calling these outlaws The Deserter Troop. Quite fittingly, we think.*

On the fourth robbery, things went bad.

This time the stage driver was armed with a holstered revolver, and the intentions to use it if the opportunity arose. And his shotgun guard was of a like mind and temperament.

The stage was carrying a sizable mine payroll, for the Jutland Brothers operation.

The troopers waited beside a road summit, watching the stage approach. They saw the driver and shotgun messenger, but did not know there was another armed guard inside the coach.

The sharp-eyed shotgun guard spotted the band lurking in the bordering greasewood and raised his weapon. Slack was about to fire at him when the concealed guard took aim and blasted Slack in the gun arm.

A firefight erupted. Slack was the first casualty of the deserters—and the last. These battle-tested troopers, tested in Arizona's deserts, knew the value of concealment and found good cover among the thick greasewood.

In five minutes the fight was over.

The stage had carried no passengers. Both the inside guard and the shotgun guard were dead, one sprawled across the coach floor, one lying facedown in the dust of the road. The driver sat slumped on his seat, blood running from his arm, a wound that had caused him to drop the handgun he grabbed from his belt when the shooting started.

"You sit tight, old man," Madden ordered, riding out of the cover of the brush. "Craig, you and Slack keep an eye on him. The rest of you, see if there's a strongbox inside there."

They obeyed his order.

Slack, despite his wound, had dismounted and picked up his gun with his left hand. His face was hard with pain. "Let me kill the son of a bitch."

"No, goddammit!" Madden said. "In this business, you don't kill the drivers unless you have to."

"Why the hell not?"

"Because they're the ones keep the stages running. You want to halt these treasure shipments?"

As they lifted the strongbox from the stage, Hiller said, "Treasure is right, by the weight of it."

"Shoot the lock off," Madden said.

"Sure thing." Hiller drew his gun and blasted away.

A couple of others grabbed at the lid and raised it.

Madden said to the driver, "How much is in there?"

"Hell, they don't tell me. But it's a mine payroll. Enough to make you thieving bastards happy."

"Watch your mouth, old man," Slack said. "I'm hurting bad enough to kill you."

The driver was trying to tie a neckerchief around his bleeding forearm, using his other hand and his teeth. He said, "This ain't no pinprick I got."

"The difference is," Slack said, "I can shoot left-handed."

"Go ahead and shoot then, damn your eyes!"

Slack raised the gun and aimed at the jehu's chest.

Craig stepped in close, grabbed Slack's arm, and held it.

"Let go, damn you!"

Madden looked up from the open strongbox sitting in the road. "Slack, I gave you an order."

For a short spell, Slack stared at him.

Madden stared back. "You want a share of what's in this box?"

There was a short silence. Then Slack said, "I reckon I do."

"Then put up that gun."

"Tell this frigging pet of yours to let me go."

Madden said, "Craig!"

Craig released Slack's arm.

Slack reached around awkwardly to holster his weapon and said, "You and me, Craig, we ain't done with this."

"So be it," Craig said.

Just before they left the scene, after they had stuffed currency into sacks they carried, Madden said to the wounded driver, "Think you can make it into Pioche, old man?"

"I'll damn sure try," the driver said. "I got one good hand, ain't I?"

"No hard feelings, old man," Madden said.

"Are you kidding?" the old man said. "I hate your goddam guts!"

On the long ride back to Chisco Springs, Madden sensed that the troopers' elation at the size of the haul began to lessen some as they realized they were now, in the eyes of the law, murderers.

Slack was in great pain from a torn muscle, though the bullet had not struck bone. And he was worried that a derelict doctor, who had recently showed at Chisco, might have moved on, leaving him with no treatment.

"I could get blood poisoning," he said once.

"They got carbolic acid at the store," Madden said. "I can treat you as well as that drunken doc."

Slack didn't answer. He went back to brooding.

Madden knew he was still fuming from his altercation with Craig.

And that was another problem, Madden thought. Some of the men were getting leery of Craig and his naysaying. He'd have to speak to him about that.

He waited though until they got back to Chisco Springs.

Luckily, the medico was still there. Unluckily, he was drunk as a skunk. Still, he retained enough of a former skill to clean and bandage Slack's torn arm.

That done, Madden took Craig aside and said, "I always figured you for a top fighting man, Raymond, based on what action I'd seen you in. Young and green as you were when you first came to Maxon, you proved yourself in a couple or three brushes against Apaches."

Craig was silent.

"That's why I picked you up off that porch at the Winn hog ranch. I figured you were too good a man to let go to hell the way you appeared to be going. But, Raymond, you let me down at the stage holdup. Me and your other comrades." He paused. "I recall you did not fire a weapon, even when the enemy opened their attack."

"That's right," Craig said.

"Why?"

"They were just doing a job they were hired to do."

"You used your weapon against those hired guns at the mine."

Craig was silent again. Then he said, "Yeah, I did. And I been sorry for it ever since."

"A man can't straddle a fence," Madden said. "Comes to a shoot-out, you got to take part."

"At seven men against three, it didn't appear you needed help," Craig said.

"If it had been three of us against seven of them, would it have made a difference?"

"Maybe," Craig said. "Sarge, this is tearing me apart inside. I want out."

Madden's face hardened. "You can't get out," he said. "You know too much now."

"I wouldn't tell anybody anything," Craig said.

"You may believe you wouldn't. But circumstances could come that would change that."

"What circumstances?"

Madden shrugged. "Who knows? But it's a risk me and the men can't afford to take."

"I don't have the stomach for robbing stagecoaches. Especially now that I see how it can lead to killing innocent men."

"It's a chance they take when they hire on as guards and drivers," Madden said.

"I want no part of it," Craig said. "It's as simple as that."

"A lot of men work at jobs they want no part of," Madden said. "It's a matter of playing out the hand that's dealt you."

"I want another deal," Craig said.

Madden shook his head. "It's too late for that. You're one of us now. Guilty enough to go to prison, if caught—hung, if taken by vigilantes. Craig, you've got no choice but to stay where your friends are."

PART II

The Predators

CHAPTER 5

CRAIG rode away in the night, with no more than a vague idea of where he would go or what he would do.

He retraced the trail to the scene of the holdup. He considered returning to Pioche, which was the only town in Nevada he knew. If he did, would the driver recognize him? After all, he, like the others, had kept his face half-hidden with a neckerchief.

A cavalry neckerchief, for chrissakes! It was as if Madden wanted his bunch to be identified. Perhaps Madden figured the military emblem would intimidate the expressmen, making the robberies easier. Maybe it had. But it added risk to Craig's possible return to the mining town, especially since he wore the brand of deserter on each hip.

If somebody started putting pieces together and pegged him as one of the bunch preying on the shipments, he could expect a lynch rope in a hurry . . . unless he could bargain information for a clean slate.

Craig knew he would never betray his old comrades, even if the mining company was willing to negotiate. He could no longer go along with Sarge, but he was grateful for the interest Madden had taken in him. He assumed Madden had looked after him because he was younger than the other troopers. Well, that was finished now, he was sure. He could imagine Madden's fury when he discovered Craig was gone.

With considerable trepidation, he turned his mount toward Pioche. There were several men in the mining town who might recall he had been riding with the troopers who had taken part in driving the usurpers from the Crowell mine. But there was a good chance no one would remember him or associate him with Madden's gang. One thing had set him apart from the others. He had been in civilian clothes and had been mounted, as he still was, on a range horse with a stock saddle.

If cornered, he would say that he had casually joined the gang on the trail up from Arizona and that he had taken part in their action at the mine only because Madden had offered him equal pay. And that he had left them when he found out what their intentions were.

The story did not seem very believable to him, but he hoped it was only because he knew the truth.

And in these mining towns, he had heard, there was a laxness about probing into another man's background. Perhaps because there were so many whose own lives could not stand scrutiny. Shady dealings went on at all levels of mine and mine stock promotion. In an area where men bought and sold mines "salted" with gold from elsewhere—planted in barren claims to fool gullible buyers—where gold and silver fever burned away common sense from men's minds, Craig hoped his story would be accepted.

He rode into town and left his mount at the livery stable for care and feeding. He headed toward the Pioche Hotel and ran into John Crowell coming toward him on the street.

Instinctively, he started to turn away in order to avoid being recognized by Crowell. But he forced himself to confront the mine owner; Craig was resolved to face up to whatever Crowell's reaction might be.

Crowell's step slowed as he approached, as did Craig's. Both men halted a few paces apart. Their eyes met, and for a time there was nothing but silence between them.

It was Crowell who spoke first. "Craig, isn't it?"

"Yes, sir," Craig said.

"You left town with that bunch of cavalry deserters."

"Yes, sir," Craig said again.

"They are all wanted men now," Crowell said.

"I have left them," Craig said.

"So it appears. Why?"

"I am not cut out to be an outlaw," Craig said.

"I see." Crowell stood silently studying him. His eyes fell to the gun in the open-top holster that Craig was wearing. "But you wear a gun well."

"I was wearing it when I helped clear out those claim jumpers for you, Mr. Crowell."

"So you were," Crowell said. "I recall it was you who was most effective in that charge into the adit."

"Circumstances caught me up in the action," Craig said. "I'm not a killer, Mr. Crowell."

"When did you leave that deserter bunch?"

"We were longtime comrades," Craig said, sudenly deciding to be truthful. "That's my excuse for not parting with them sooner. They were men I had fought Apaches with. First Sergeant Madden was a man I respected. He picked me up after I had been unjustly branded a deserter myself and driven out of the army with no place to go." He paused. "He was a friend to me. Almost like a father, really."

"And now?" Craig said.

"I want no part of them. I'm looking for a job."

"You say you were branded a deserter yourself?"

"I was. Unjustly."

"Tell me about it."

"It happened several weeks before the others deserted," Craig said. "It's kind of a long story, Mr. Crowell."

"I've got time to listen. Come on to the saloon and I'll buy you a drink."

When Craig finished his account of being drummed out of the army and rescued from his drunken stupor by Madden, Crowell said, "That's some story—if it's true."

"You don't believe me?"

"I guess I do," Crowell said. "Enough that I'll give you a job on the basis of your action in driving out those highgraders earlier. According to Madden, it was your fast shooting that gave us a quick victory."

"I am not a killer for hire, Mr. Crowell."

"I don't believe you are. But you handle weapons well. At least that Colt you carry. If you are agreeable, I can put you on as one of my mine guards. Regular shifts at moderate pay." Crowell paused, then said, "But I must warn you there is always a possibility you will have to use your gun to protect our properties. Pioche is rife with would-be claim jumpers, and we have other claims besides the Worthington and Crowell. You might be called upon to defend any of our sites."

Craig was silent.

Crowell's face showed a trace of impatience. "Do you want the job or don't you?" he said.

"Yes, sir. I reckon I do," Craig said finally. "Just so you know I ain't a killer for hire."

"Report tomorrow morning at my office," Crowell said.

Craig was placed on solitary guard duty at the mouth of the shaft where he and Madden and the others had stormed the claim encroachers' hirelings. According to Crowell there had been no further trouble since that date, although a guard had been on duty ever since.

Craig took over a shift just vacated by a man who had gone elsewhere, for reasons not given to Craig. The job was boring, but at least it was honest work. Still, he wondered how long he could stand a steady diet of it.

In the army there had been a daily routine of various tasks. Here, it was everlasting sentry duty, to which he was not temperamentally suited. Despite his dislike of killing, he had always welcomed the occasional patrol with its ever-present threat of dangerous Apache confrontation.

There could be some threat here too, he told himself, and that may have been the reason for Crowell's hiring him.

Pioche was now southeastern Nevada's richest and most important mining camp, but it was also its most notorious for lawlessness. Now in its third or fourth year of serious development, it was still a hotbed of conflict among claimants.

Many claim controversies were taken to the overworked courts, but more were settled by gunmen. Word had gone out about this, and Pioche had become a magnet for hired guns and thugs of every caliber.

And what am I, Craig thought ruefully, *if not one of them?*

On the night of September 15, disaster struck the town.

It was the eve of Mexico's independence day, and the Mexican workers of the town set out to celebrate with street dancing, bonfires, drinking, and singing. Just past midnight, flames burst from the rear of a diner on the upper part of Main Street.

Before the inhabitants could even attempt to extinguish it, the fire had leaped to adjoining structures built of dry, inflammable materials. The onrushing flames swept the buildings away in quick succession, leaving only heaps of ashes and burning embers of what an hour before had been the leading mining town of the district.

Three hundred kegs of blasting powder, stored in the cellar of a leading mercantile house on Main Street, exploded with a force that shook the surroundings for miles around. Rocks, timbers, and every type of debris swept across Main and Meadow Valley Streets; the watchers on the latter street were raked as if by wartime grape and canister.

Thirteen men were killed and forty-seven others were seriously wounded. Two thousand people had lost their shelters or their business places.

Craig was just into his first hour of the "graveyard" tour of his guard duty when the fire began.

From up there on the slope, he had an immediate view of it. His first inclination was to run down the hill to give alarm, but he could see that people already were in the streets, some

running around in panic, others milling about in shock. A
few tried futilely to combat the fire.

Around him he saw guards from the other nearby mines
running down the slope toward the conflagration, and his
compulsion to follow returned.

He stayed behind because of his army training: a sentry
does not abandon his post.

Down in the town, two armed men had trouble keeping their
satisfaction from showing on their faces. They stood side by
side on the fringe of a crowd, and now one nudged the
other. "Time to go, Sam."

Sam nodded, and followed his partner as he led the way
unobtrusively toward the slope of Treasure Hill, where the
mines were.

"Hey Driscoll, you reckon that guard up there come down
to see the burning?" Sam asked.

"I seen some of them from the other mines come down.
I'd guess it would leastwise distract him, which was our
intent. Give our boys a chance to crack Crowell's office safe
without being noticed."

"I rather be up there, my own self. Them boys get that
safe open, they just might take off with our shares."

"Let's get up there," Sam said. And they hurried off,
unnoticed by the panicked crowd.

Crowell's mine office was fifty yards from the shaft entrance,
one of several utility structures clustered above and a little to
one side of the adit.

It was a moonless night, and the grouped buildings formed
a dark mass against the terrain.

Craig, turning for brief respite from staring at the fire
below, was startled as his eyes seemed to catch a momentary
glint of light from within a window. For a second, he attrib-
uted it to his eyes adjusting from the glare of the fire below.

But that couldn't be, he thought. The distance from the inferno was too great to cause his eyes to play tricks on him.

For a considerable time he studied the darkened structures, particularly the spot where he judged the office to be. Again he thought he glimpsed a moment of interior light, as of a match lit and suddenly extinguished.

Someone was in the office. Could it be Crowell? At this time of night?

Hardly likely. If Crowell were making a midnight check, he would have stopped by Craig's sentry post before venturing further, if for no other reason than to avoid alarm.

He then felt driven to investigate and moved forward up the incline. He drew his gun and tried not to make a sound.

Sam stopped so suddenly that Driscoll bumped into him.

"What the hell—?" Driscoll grumbled.

"Shut up, goddammit! I seen somebody move away from the mine." Sam stared ahead into the darkness.

Driscoll thought he also saw a shadow figure moving up toward the buildings. As the figure disappeared, he said in a low tone, "Damn guard must have stuck by his post. Now what?"

"Must have heard or seen the boys up there," Sam said.

"We got to warn them."

"How?" Sam said.

Driscoll made no answer.

After a moment, Sam said, "We got to get on up there. Come on!"

He started off fast and kicked loose some scattered slag.

"Jeez!" Driscoll said, under his breath.

They paused, listening to hear if the sound had reached the guard.

Neither could tell.

"We got to go on," Sam whispered.

"Why?"

"For the money, you damn fool."

"I ain't so sure," Driscoll said.

But Sam had gone ahead, picking his way carefully now. Driscoll hesitated, then moved out after him.

Craig thought he heard someone many yards behind him. Briefly, he was tugged by a desire to know who they were, but his curiosity concerning the light he'd glimpsed in Crowell's office took precedence.

He reached the office door, twisted the knob slowly, found it unlocked, and opened the door a bare crack.

At that moment a match flared within, and a man's deep voice said, "Light one of them candles you're carrying. I got to see the damn dial. Just listening to the tumblers ain't doing the job."

The light strengthened as the candle wick took the flame.

Peering in, Craig could see two men hunkered in front of the office safe, one apparently working the dial, the other holding the candle.

Both men wore casual street clothes, and revolvers on their hips.

Hired guns, Craig guessed.

He saw the man at the safe pull open the iron door, then reach in for the contents.

An awkward position to draw from, Craig thought, and made his move, flinging the office door partially open. He leveled his gun at the man with the candle, who was now standing, and said, "Don't move!"

The man at the safe jerked around and made a wild grab for his gun.

At the same time the other man dropped the candle and reached for his holster. Craig shot him dead. He landed beside the still burning candle and his greasy clothing caught fire.

The man at the safe had made an awkward draw and shot wildly; his bullet ripped away part of the door jamb at the level of Craig's head.

Craig fired back and the safecracker sprawled unmoving, blood gushing from a hole in his throat.

Almost at once the dry wood floor added fuel to the fire. In a moment the flames had risen knee high, and Craig rushed inside to fight them, giving only a quick glance at the bodies to verify they were dead. He noticed a long, protective cloak, the kind officials sometimes wore when making mine inspections, hanging from a coat tree. He snatched it from the hanger and began beating at the flames.

Outside, the two arsonists had drawn close, trying to find out whether their partners had killed the guard, yet leery in case they hadn't.

Driscoll said, "By God, Sam, there's a fire in there."

They could see the flare beyond the window.

By the time they neared the doorway, Craig had beat out the last of the flames. Choking from the smoke he made a rush for the door.

Just before he stepped out he saw the two figures coming toward him. He slipped to one side and waited.

They came close and tried to see within.

In the starshine he saw the glint of their weapons.

"Don't move!" Craig said. "And drop those guns!"

Startled, they obeyed instantly. Thinking quickly, Sam said, "We was just curious about the fire. We were just passing by on our way to the Ophir mine where we're late to relieve the guard."

"Yeah, we heard some shooting," Driscoll added.

Craig said, "There's a desk by that window in here. Ought to be a lamp on it. One of you find it and get it lit."

"Sure, friend."

"I just killed two men," Craig said. "Watch you don't try any tricks."

"Jeez! We was just passing by."

"Get that lamp lit!" Craig said.

A match flared over by the desk as Sam found the lamp and lit it.

The two firebugs stared at the bodies. Driscoll's stare returned to the one that was partly scorched. He seemed unable to take his eyes from it.

"Looks like they were robbing the safe," Sam said.

"I reckon so," Craig said.

"They got it open," Sam said. "I wonder how much they almost got."

"Bring it over and lay it on the desktop," Craig said.

Craig was watching him closely; Sam noticed this and took care as he moved toward the safe that he did nothing to set off that threatening gun again. Two accomplices of his were dead, and he wanted to make damned sure he didn't join them.

He came back to the desk and dropped a single packet of greenbacks on it.

"Count it," Craig said. "Out loud."

It came to two hundred dollars.

"Wasn't worth the killing," Sam said.

"They should have thought of that," Craig said.

"We got to get on up to the Ophir," Sam said.

"All right," Craig said. "I'll just stay here until Crowell shows up. Only be a few hours."

Out of Craig's sight, the two arsonists turned down the hill.

Sam said, "By God, we burned down half the town for a share of two hundred dollars. Which we didn't even get."

"Well," Driscoll said, "at least them poor celebrating Mexicans will be the ones that get the blame for it."

CHAPTER 6

THERE were several reports of holdups by the Deserter Troop as they terrorized the region.

From as far away as the state capital, Carson City, came a story in the *Nevada Tribune:*

> *Eastern Nevada's flourishing mining area has been lately hit by a series of stage robberies performed with military dispatch by what has become known in that area as the Deserter Troop, made up of, it is believed, several army deserters believed to have fled from service in Arizona.*
>
> *Rumor has it that military action from the Fort Halleck army garrison is being demanded by the mining interests in the vicinity to run down and apprehend these outlaw soldiers.*
>
> *Fort Halleck was established five years ago on Cottonwood Creek, thirty miles southeast of the railroad town of Elko, to subdue recalcitrant Shoshone, Paiute, and Gosiute Indian raiders. The fort is the closest army post to the area of depredations of these outlaws, but nonetheless is still nearly two hundred miles from the Pioche mining district whose payrolls have been consistently hit.*
>
> *The Halleck garrison presently consists of Company I, First United States Cavalry, who are lately kept busy by pesky Gosiutes preying on livestock of area ranchers.*
>
> *Major William Forrest is commander of the fort, and word is that he is under intense pressure by the mining corporations, some of whom it is said have Eastern political connections, to provide escorts for all stages running between the mines and the railheads.*
>
> *We would not like to be in the boots of the harassed post commander.*

Perhaps the strongest call for help came from the *Reese River Reveille* in Austin, whose editor at this time was a man who had once commanded volunteers sent out to quell an early disturbance by Paiutes and had never forgotten the experience:

> *There is a group of turncoats who are using the training given them in the profession of arms to prey upon those they once swore to protect. What better force to combat their despicable acts than those, equally trained, who have remained true to their pledge of allegiance? I speak of those of the garrison at Fort Halleck.*
>
> *It is our belief that the soldiers stationed there would gladly undertake the mission. Surely they must feel the embarrassment of knowing a rogue bunch of their own is ravaging the Sagebrush State we so proudly hail.*
>
> *I say, Major Forrest, give your soldiers the order to action against these black sheep, and you will have occasion to be proud, as will we civilians, some of who have once commanded troops ourselves.*
>
> *Signed,*
> *Joseph E. Hadley, Editor*
> *(Former Major of Volunteers)*

CHAPTER 7

AT Fort Halleck, Major William Forrest, tired of fielding demands that he do something about the outlaw deserters, and unable to offer stagecoach and express escorts for the numerous shipments on the roads, appealed to higher command for a solution to his problem.

For a time, nothing came of his appeal.

Then, he learned through the army grapevine that Fort Maxon was to be deactivated.

He at once sent a message to its post commander:

10 September 1872

From: Major Wm. Forrest
Fort Halleck, Nevada

To: Capt. Brandon Falk
Post Commander
Fort Maxon, Arizona Territory

It has come to my attention that your post is about to be deactivated and that such action may afford you an opportunity to request a transfer to a post of your choice, though of course such a request is by no means certain of being granted.

However, due to the peculiar circumstances existing here in the vicinity of Fort Halleck, a request for posting to this installation might be of singular benefit to both our careers, and you could be assured of my every cooperation in an effort to accomplish such transfer. Since we are acquainted from past service together, I feel you may be interested in my explanation for this.

You may or may not have heard of the notorious so-called Deserter Troop now preying on mine payroll and bullion shipments in this part of Nevada.

There is great pressure being put on this command to take action to end these assaults. However, our resources are such that a solution has not been forthcoming.

Which brings me to the point of this communique: It is now believed that this Deserter Troop, variously described as comprised of six to eight men, is a squad of deserters from your own post there at Maxon.

They are led by former First Sergeant Madden, according to a mine manager of Pioche who hired them several months ago, and who has given statements that at that time they were still in uniform and described themselves as recently discharged.

If this rings a bell with you, Falk, and knowing your obsession with severe punishment for violations of army regulations, it occurs to me that you might welcome a chance to mete out your own punishment to these offenders.

If so, I can put in your command a squad to make this possible.

If you are interested, and will make request for duty at this location, I will work from this end to try to get your request granted.

I will stress through channels that this action could relieve the criticism by the Nevada newspapers and the pressure put upon the army by mining and express company officials, and may forstall political appeal to Washington.

> Major Wm. Forrest
> Post Commander, Fort Halleck

> *17 September 1872*

> From: Capt. B. Falk
> Fort Maxon, Arizona Territory

To: Major Wm. Forrest
Post Commander
Fort Halleck, Nevada

In answer to your proposal, I will take steps toward its acceptance at this end.

I hope your own efforts, combined with mine, will result in its accomplishment.

*If so, I look forward to the challenge of bringing those who defy
military discipline to their just punishment.*

Captain Brandon Falk
Post Commander, Fort Maxon

Reading Falk's reply, Major Forrest frowned. It had just
occurred to him what Falk's idea of "just" punishment would
probably be.

Knowing Falk, he was certain Falk's intention would be to
personally administer the death penalty.

Nothing else would satisfy the man.

That's the way Falk was.

Once the decision was made to deactivate Fort Maxon, it had
been done with uncustomary dispatch. In a matter of a few
weeks the post was closed, its enlisted personnel and officers
distributed elsewhere, and Captain Brandon Falk on his way
to Nevada. He traveled via stage from Winn Station to Min-
eral Park, Arizona, then north into Nevada and through St.
Thomas, St. Joseph, and finally to Pioche. There, by chance,
he had a two-day stopover while he waited for a stage up to
Wells where he could catch the Central Pacific westward to
Halleck Station, twenty-odd miles northwest of the fort.

He had been riding stages for over three hundred miles
and welcomed a bath and rest in the Pioche Hotel. He had
been post-bound at Maxon for a considerable period, and
stage travel took some getting used to, he thought. Well, soon
enough he'd be in the saddle, getting toughened up again in
pursuit of those goddam deserters.

That was a thought that allayed his present discomfort
considerably. The warm bath, a good meal, and a night's
sleep eased it even more.

The next morning he went out to study the town, of which
he had recently heard from Major Forrest, since it was one
of the mining centers most directly victimized by his incipient

quarry. When he walked outside he was startled to see someone walking down the main street who looked familiar. The man's back was now toward him. Falk did not hesitate; he walked fast enough to overtake the sauntering figure, and when he was close enough he spoke.

"Hold on there!" he said with such authority that the man halted.

Raymond Craig turned. His eyes grew bitter as recognition came. "Well, Falk," he said, "I'm beyond your reach now."

Falk's glance went to Craig's holstered gun. He remained silent.

"What do you want, *sir?*" Craig said.

The sardonic tone enraged Falk, but he kept control. "Nothing in particular, soldier. I just arrived in town, and happened to see you going by. I thought I'd speak my feelings. I bear you no ill feelings, despite your conduct at Maxon. You paid for what you did." He paused. "Are you hiring out that gun you wear?"

"None of your business, is it?"

Falk held a thoughtful look. "I was hoping you wouldn't bear a grudge. What happened was a result of your infraction of military regulations. Nothing personal on my part."

"Of course not, Captain."

"If there is no grudge," Falk said, "I may be able to offer you employment."

"Grudge?" Craig gave a short laugh. "Captain, I hate your guts."

Falk's eyes narrowed. "That hog-ranch owner at Winn's Station told me you rode off with a bunch led by Madden," Falk said quickly. "I'm curious just where the others are."

"You'll learn nothing from me," Craig said.

"They are that wild bunch that's preying on express shipments up here, aren't they?"

"You don't know that."

"You do, though, don't you?"

"Let me ask you a question, Captain," Craig said. "What are you doing in Nevada?"

"I've been ordered to Fort Halleck."

Craig showed interest, but only said, "God help the garrison there."

Falk scowled.

"What happened at Maxon?" Craig asked. "The higher brass get wise to your methods when your own first sergeant led part of your troops away?"

"Fort Maxon was deactivated," Falk said.

"You were that poor an officer, eh?"

"It was a matter of War Department cost cutting."

Suspicion struck at Craig. "You *asked* for duty at Halleck, I'll bet!" He paused. "Losing those deserters must have had something to do with the closing of your post. No doubt, you're out for revenge against Madden and his bunch. A man like you must have found the desertions hard to take."

"They are preying on the public interests," Falk said, "and they have to be stopped. Since the law authorities have been unable to stop them, the military has been called in."

"Meaning you?"

"Meaning me," Falk said. "And despite your violation of military regulations, I assume you are a law-abiding civilian. So I would hope you would give me any help you can to apprehend these deserter road agents."

"Not to the likes of you," Craig said.

"I'm guessing that gun you're wearing is now your means of livelihood."

"So what if it is?"

"You are either one of two things. You are an outlaw, or you are in the hire of one of the mining companies. Either way, I can cause you trouble."

"In what way?"

"Well, if you are an outlaw, say one of Madden's bunch placed here in town to tip him off to treasure shipments, there are plenty of late-paid miners ready to hang you."

"I'm employed by one of the companies as a mine guard," Craig said. "Honest employment. I have nothing to do with payroll or other shipments."

"And how would your honest employer feel about you if he knew you were drummed out of the army in disgrace?"

"Same old Falk," Craig said.

"Right," Falk said. "And you'd best remember that."

"I'm not likely to forget."

"No, I guess not. Those brands are a long time healing, I've been told."

"As far as I'm concerned, Captain, they'll never heal."

"Look, there's no need for me to go to your employer, if you'll cooperate with me."

"Madden and his men were my comrades, Captain. But I don't suppose you'd understand the way I feel."

"Right is right," Falk said. "Wrong is wrong. That's the way I see things."

"And who decides what's right, Captain? You?"

"Exactly."

"I happen to disagree."

"You may change your mind," Falk said.

"It won't be you that makes me."

"We'll see about that," Falk said.

Craig turned and walked away. He could feel Falk's stare following him, and he cursed silently. Falk could make trouble for him. . . .

It took some inquiring around before Falk could learn where Craig was employed. When he did, he immediately got directions to the Worthington & Crowell office, and went there.

John Crowell admitted him, scowling as he glanced at the uniform. "About time the army sent somebody here to investigate what's going on," he said.

"I have been told your company has been one of the victims," Falk said.

"Yes, by God! And each time by that goddamned bunch of deserters."

"You have one of them in your employ."

"Craig? He's different. He did a good job for me when he first arrived here. And he left the bunch as soon as they turned outlaw."

"He was a lone deserter," Falk said, "before any of the rest."

"He told me what happened. When he came to me after leaving the others."

"Did you know he was branded? With the army D for deserter?"

"Undeservedly, as I understand it. All because he tried to save a child from Apaches. Some sadistic son of a bitch of an officer ordered it."

Falk's face flushed. He said, "I was that officer. And there was nothing sadistic about it. He violated orders and paid the penalty for it."

Crowell gave him a long, searching look, then said, "Well, sometimes there are two sides to a story. Why have you come to me?"

"I am on detached duty to put an end to the deserter robberies."

"Yes?"

"Ex-Private Craig is familiar with their habits."

"Craig is a good man," Crowell said, "regardless of his background."

"He could be of good use in running down the predators. He might prove invaluable to my force."

"Hell, you're the one put the hot iron to him!" Crowell said. "He's got a job here, why would he help you?"

"He's in your hire. You fire him, and I'll hire him at civilian scout's pay to guide me."

"Captain, you are a bastard!" Crowell said. "There are two things wrong with your reasoning. One, the man is serving me well in the job I've given him, and I will not fire him.

Second, you'd never get him to scout for you, not against his old associates."

"Why not?" Falk said. "He left the bunch of his own accord, apparently. For whatever reason."

"And I know that reason," John Crowell said. "It was because he couldn't abide a life of crime."

"All the more reason he should help stop them."

Crowell gave him another studying look. "I guess you find it hard to understand loyalty to friends. I can see why. You strike me as a man who probably never had any."

"I understand loyalty to law and regulations," Falk said. "That supersedes any other kind, in my book."

"After the treatment Craig got from you, he undoubtedly feels differently."

"Let me lay it out in black and white," Falk said. "If you want the robberies stopped, you'll cooperate with me."

"I'll think about it," Crowell said.

"Now! Fire him now, and I'll take him with me to Fort Halleck."

"I doubt that," Crowell said. "But I will not be pressured by you into a rush decision on any account."

Falk showed anger at being rebuffed. "You may well regret it!"

"Not if the army does its job," Crowell said. "Besides, you must have a scout or two at Halleck who knows this terrain."

"Quite possibly," Falk said. "But none who knows that bunch of deserters and their haunts."

"I said I'd think about it."

"That may make it too late."

"So be it," John Crowell said.

Falk left Crowell's office, raging inwardly. The relative autonomy of an isolated post command had accustomed him to having his wishes carried out without objection. Dealing with a hardheaded civilian with ideas of his own was something for which he had low tolerance.

It would serve the son of a bitch right if the deserters

struck his next payroll, Falk thought. Maybe that would bring him around to listening to good suggestions when he heard them. Right now, Captain Falk wouldn't have lifted a finger to stop Crowell cash from being taken, and this in spite of his own driving desire to wipe out Madden and his deserters.

And wipe them out he would.

He'd do it, not because of their pillaging of mining-company money or bullion. Nor to relieve the pressure on the army at Fort Halleck. And certainly not to remove public criticism from the epauletted shoulders of Major William Forrest, with whom he had once been a fellow lieutenant and whom he now envied because Forrest had advanced to a higher rank.

He'd do it as a matter of vengeance against Madden and those other low-life bastards who had dared to desert his command. Of course there could be side benefits to himself when he accomplished his dedicated mission. It could impress the War Department brass, hopefully leading to another post command.

Perhaps, he thought, even at Fort Halleck. The idea intrigued him. He might end up replacing Forrest, who had apparently been unsuccessful at coping with the problem that excited the Nevada press.

There were possibilities here—that same critical press could make him a hero. Or at least give him widespread fame as a spectacular officer. The thought fed his vanity, made him eager to get started on the task.

He saw no point at present in wasting any more effort trying to persuade Craig or Crowell to his way of thinking. Now he was impatient with the wait for the stage to take him toward Halleck.

Eventually it arrived, and he embarked with five other passengers without hearing further from Crowell. All right, he thought, let the bastard take the consequences of not listening to a good suggestion.

The stagecoach rocked and swayed on the thoroughbraces

as the driver kept the team moving at a good pace. But the discomfort of the ride scarcely touched him as his mind went over the details of his plan of action.

His whole being screamed for a personal encounter with that rogue first sergeant and his traitorous bunch.

He'd show them they couldn't desert a command of his and not pay the ultimate penalty. Hopefully, he, Falk, could find a chance to dispatch that son of a bitch Madden personally.

At that moment, his thoughts were interrupted as the driver abruptly pulled in the team.

Then Falk heard a voice from the side of the road. It was familiar, but it took a few seconds for him to place it. His hand went at once to his holstered revolver; he unloosened the flap, drew the weapon.

Immediately, two burly miner passengers, one on either side, grabbed at the gun. The stronger one wrested it from his grip.

"Don't you be doing anything foolish, Captain," the other said.

"So! You two are with them," Falk said harshly.

"Not at all," one said. "But you'll start them shooting, if you show that gun. And if they start, we'll likely all end up dead."

"Cowards!" Falk said.

"But live ones," the first miner said. "I don't aim to die to save the reputation of a stage line."

"They'll rob you," Falk said.

"So what have I got to lose? A week's pay."

The driver, top-side, shouted down, "You fellers best step out. It's that goddam deserter troop again."

Falk and five other passengers disembarked, their hands raised above their heads.

Falk stared up at the mounted men, whose faces were covered with the yellow neckerchiefs he'd heard had become their trademark.

Only random pieces of their uniforms remained, most of them replaced by range rider clothing. What remained were trooper hats, cavalry boots, and the McClellan saddles. About half of them still rode U.S. branded horses.

He could identify at once three of them from their builds and postures.

Three besides Madden, whose voice had already identified him.

"Geezchrize!" one of the deserters said. "Look what the hell we got here, Sarge."

"Morning, Captain, sir," Madden's voice said.

Falk was silent.

"Hope you are carrying a fair amount of pocket money, sir," Madden said.

Still Falk said nothing.

"Let me shoot the son of a bitch," one of the others said.

"Why?" Madden said.

"For old times sake, Sarge. For the memories he brings to mind, just seeing the son of a bitch."

"He's harmless to us now," Madden said. "No reason to shed his blood." He paused, then addressed Falk again. "What are you doing here in Nevada, sir?"

"Transfer to Fort Halleck," Falk said.

"I heard they closed Fort Maxon," Madden said. "But isn't it a kind of coincidence, you being transferred up here where we are?"

"Yes, it is," Falk said.

"Is it, Captain?" Madden turned to his men and said, "A couple of you dismount and see they clean out their pockets. The rest of you keep them covered and shoot if they make a wrong move." He paused. "Start with the captain."

Two dismounted and began a brusque search of Falk, including patting him down for a concealed weapon. All they turned up were his wallet and his orders to Fort Halleck.

One of them tossed the wallet up to Madden, who opened it.

There were a couple of hundred dollars inside, in green-backs.

"All of us are making more pay now than you are, it appears," Madden said. "Don't that make you feel envious, Captain?"

Falk did not reply.

"Dammit, Captain, when I speak to you I expect an answer!"

"Let me shoot the son of a bitch," the trooper who had spoken earlier said again. He raised his sidearm and pointed it at Falk's chest.

Falk said quickly, "No, I don't envy you."

"Let me see those papers he's carrying," Madden said to the man who was holding them.

They were handed to him, and he scanned them quickly. He looked down then at the scowling captain. "Detached duty, eh, sir? And what would that be meaning, I wonder."

"No concern of yours," Falk said.

Madden did not speak at once. When he did, he said, "I'm wondering about that, Captain."

The driver, still on his seat, had been taking in the conversation, along with the other passengers. Now, he said, "Listen, I got a schedule to keep. You boys mind getting done with your business so I can get along?"

"Get done with it, men," Madden said. "We want to keep the jehu there happy." He nodded toward the driver.

There was a pile of wallets, watches, rings, and coins in the roadway.

"Small pickings," one of the robbers said. "Let's see what the driver's got."

"No," Madden said. "You know the rule—we don't rob the drivers. Can't you get that through your head?"

"But this time the pickings are slim, Sarge."

"Makes no difference, dammit!" Madden said. "Pick up the take and stow it in your saddlebags."

The one who had protested did so, grumbling.

This was too much for Captain Falk to ignore. "You see, Sergeant, without the U.S. Army behind you, you're nothing. You thought you were big, but now you've got men resisting your orders. That's another argument for my belief in hard discipline, enforced by regulations."

"I do better than you would in my place, Captain," he said.

"I would never be in your place," Falk said. "I am a man who believes in order. You've chosen a life of anarchy. You will increasingly find that anarchy destroys itself." He paused, then said, "Your days are numbered, Madden."

"Is that a threat, Captain? If I thought you meant it personally, I ought to shoot you now."

"Let me do it for you," the trigger-happy robber said.

This time, Madden was slow to answer, as if he were considering. Finally, he said, "No. If you murder an army officer in cold blood, it could cause repercussions that we don't need."

"You getting soft, Sarge?"

"I'm telling you how it is!" Madden said. "I don't want any arguing, you hear?"

His eyes were still on Falk, and he saw a faint sign of amusement that Falk made no attempt to hide.

"You see, Sergeant?" Falk said. "You've got the early signs of rebellion there. That's what happens when you flaunt rules and regulations. You've got a band of anarchists with you now. You can expect trouble to grow in your control of them."

"I don't need any lectures from you," Madden said.

The driver spoke up again. "You got what loot there is. Can I get rolling now?"

"Go ahead," Madden said. Then he addressed Falk. "I was hoping, Captain, that I'd never see you again."

Falk was getting into the stage as the driver took hold of the reins. He looked back over his shoulder and said, "I haven't been sharing that hope, Sergeant." He got into the coach, slamming the door.

The driver got the team moving at a fast pace.

Madden sat his horse, staring after them. He thought belatedly, *I wonder what he meant by that.*

CHAPTER 8

MAJOR Forrest came out of his headquarters office at Fort Halleck to greet Captain Falk. Although Forrest seemed glad to see him, overly so, Falk sensed his smoldering dislike. Falk could understand the major's feeling, because he felt the same emotions, even as they shook hands.

It had always been like this between them.

Falk almost smiled, realizing how badly Forrest needed him. Otherwise, the major would never have suggested he try for the transfer.

The man was desperate, Falk thought, and he relished the fact because it gave him an edge. An edge that might be used to level the difference in rank between them.

A quick glance at the cantonment as he had been driven in had shown Falk that Fort Halleck was an improvement over Fort Maxon. Now five years old, it had been built at the base of the Ruby Mountains, its purpose at that time to protect the railroad construction workers against attacks by Paiute, Shoshone, and Gosiute Indians.

Around the parade ground were the enlisted men's barracks built of adobe and logs, as was a storehouse. There was a board-covered surgeon's quarters adjacent to a two-story hospital, and beyond were the stables, blacksmith shop, bakery, kitchen, and mess hall.

Nearer the headquarters structure were verandahed officers' quarters of board frame and adobe, nestled among plantings of cottonwoods.

Now, with the railroad long completed, the fort's garrison had been drastically cut, although Major Forrest still had a nearly full company of cavalry.

Knowing this, Falk had some wonder why Forrest could not spare enough men to escort the various stage and freight wagons plying the eastern Nevada routes. It was a question he was driven to ask almost at once, as Forrest led him into his office.

Forrest, a ruddy-faced, stocky man in his mid-thirties, with graying hair, held back a frown. He accepted the bluntness of the question as another expression of Falk's critical attitude toward his command ability. He had a brief moment of regret that he had ever contacted Falk about the possibility of a transfer.

But when he answered, he showed no offense. "This is not the best of times for us. There was a period of quiet once the railroad was finished, I am told. Lately, though, the tribes have renewed their offenses."

"Offenses?" Falk said. "You mean offensives?"

"So far they are better described as offenses. Minor, scattered raids on isolated ranches. Horse and stock stealing. The steady increase of the offenses, though, leads me to believe they are leading up to a full-blown offensive in the near future.

"To answer your question, though, I will say that the frequency of their depredations keeps my men almost continuously in the field. We are the only major army installation here in eastern Nevada. In western Utah for that matter, until you get to Fort Douglas near Salt Lake.

"So you called on me," Falk said, "Why?"

"Probably for the same reason you responded," Forrest said. "I believe you have a deeper motivation than any other officer in the army would have in this particular situation." He met Falk's stare and said, "Am I right?"

"You read a man well," Falk said.

"In your case, I think so. You are outraged by the desertion of your first sergeant with a squad of your troops," Major Forrest said. "You have taken personal offense at the action.

Nothing this side of personal vengeance will satisfy your outrage."

Falk's eyes probed at him. "If it had happened to you, would you have felt any differently? I mean it's a matter of record, likely discussed over drinks by officers and enlisted men alike wherever they meet. Every commander in the frontier army has lost men by desertions, but do you know of any aside from myself who has lost a first sergeant with them?"

"Frankly, no. Although it may have happened." Forrest paused. "At any rate, as I said, you have a personal motive that no one else would have for running down these culprits. And that's why I welcome you to Fort Halleck, Captain."

"You are using me, Major."

"Exactly," Forrest said. "Do you object?"

"I do not like to be used. But in this case I make an exception."

"I felt certain you would."

"I can't do it alone, of course."

"I can spare you a squad," Forrest said. "For as long as it takes." He paused. "Unless, of course, the Indian trouble worsens."

"So you are really expecting that?" Falk said.

Forrest shrugged. "You never know about the Indians up here. They are not like your Arizona Apaches. A different breed entirely. Not consistent in their fight against the whites. For one thing, they do not have leaders like Cochise or Mangas Coloradas. In the Pyramid Lake War in the sixties, they had the Paiute chief, Numaga, one of their best, and they whipped the whites there decisively. Later, there were small uprisings by lesser chiefs, Black Rock Tom, also a Paiute, and a couple of years later a renegade Shoshone named Big Foot, up in Paradise Valley.

"But most of the trouble in recent years has been from small bands with unknown leaders. Now, though, since I've been here, we have been troubled by one called Lone Horse, a Gosiute who is rumored to be in contact with leaders among the Paiutes and Western Shoshones. I've heard that he seeks to gather them into a single force. If so, it could be for the purpose of a major attack."

Falk said, "What is his complaint?"

Forrest said, "This is a pretty barren country for them to exist in. Hunting is poor because grazing is sparse. There is scant game, and that only in the mountain valleys, many of which have been taken over by white ranchers. Most of the Indians have to live on the small creatures of the sagebrush flats and hills and deserts. Rabbits and rats, for God's sake."

"You sound like an Indian-lover," Falk said. "If you will allow me to be frank, Major."

"Well, frankly, I'm not. Still, there is something to say in their defense. Try living on rabbits and rats, Captain."

"That's all?"

"No. A big staple of their diet has always been the pine nuts gathered each autumn from the piñon forests in the mountains. Unfortunately, the proliferation of mines in recent years is destroying that supply. Trees are cut down for mine timbers. The piñon forests are being destroyed to supply the kilns that make the charcoal used to fuel the reduction mills that process silver and gold ore.

"At first it was scarcely noticeable, I suppose. But now, with boom after boom in eastern Nevada mining, the pine nut source is being eradicated. The Indians are being driven to desperation.

"The time is ripe for an uprising," Forrest said. "At least that is my fear."

Falk said, "Damned Indians' complaint is always the same. On the plains, it is the buffalo being killed off that they use as an excuse for their atrocities. Now, pine nuts?"

Forrest frowned. "At any rate, this brings us back to why my garrison is busy."

"And gives me the problem of the deserters," Falk said. "A

problem I intend to solve. But you must give me a free hand to do so, Major."

"You will have it."

Falk's first request of Forrest was to see the records of likely prospects for his squad.

"I may be able to narrow it down for you," the major said. "Like any troop commander, I have some idea of the potentials of the men under me."

"To put it simply," Falk said, "I want good soldiers. And I'd like men you think would be willing to shoot down deserters."

"I would be satisfied if you took them prisoner," the major said, "brought them in to be tried."

Falk's face grew hard. "But I wouldn't," he said. "You recall, Major, that you agreed I can do this my own way."

"Perhaps I shouldn't have." Forrest paused. "The type of men you are suggesting aren't necessarily the best soldiers. They tend to chafe under discipline, just like the men you are about to hunt down."

"I will handle that," Falk said. "Discipline is a specialty of mine."

"You seem to have failed with the bunch you are going after."

"Only because of a renegade first sergeant who led them astray, apparently for reasons of his own."

"Very well," Forrest said. "I will go over the roster with you and try to describe briefly each man's qualifications for what I think you want."

"Six men only," Falk said.

"Six?"

"The first sergeant took six men with him," Falk said.

"There is the first sergeant himself."

"With whom I intend to deal personally," Falk said.

"You seem to be making this into some sort of a game."

"It is, and one I am going to enjoy more if the sides are even."

They were in the headquarters office, and Forrest laid a copy of the roster on his desk between them.

He said, "I'll read off the names of the men I can spare who I think may suit your requirements. I will give you a brief rundown on what might be their qualifications. Let me know your own opinions."

Falk nodded.

Forrest scanned part way down the list before he read a name aloud.

"Private Barlow." he said. He paused, as if mentally summing up an appraisal of the man. "Second enlistment. Age thirty. Average soldier, but, having served most of his prior enlistment at this post, has considerable knowledge of the terrain."

"I'll take him," Falk said.

Forrest scanned further.

"Private Reed. Three years in the service. Age, early twenties. Likes action, slightly wounded twice. Occasional company punishment for minor infractions, usually it seems as a result of boredom during a period when the redskins were relatively quiet."

"Taken," Falk said.

"Private Wilkes. Late thirties. Background unknown. In fourth year of enlistment. Good soldier in garrison, good in the field. Possible corporal material, were we in need of one."

"Taken."

Forest looked up from the roster and said. "No objections, Falk?"

"None so far," Falk said.

"I'm rather surprised," Forrest said, and dropped his eyes to the roster again.

"Private Starkey. Also in second enlistment. Plus two years of early army service."

The major looked up again.

Falk said, "What do you mean by that?"

"Confederate army," Forrest said. "A Texan."

"I thought you knew how I felt about ex-rebels in our frontier army," Falk said.

"Yes, I recall," Forrest said. "Which is why I brought him up. I wanted to see if you still bore your prejudice."

"I do."

"He is a seasoned fighting man. Went back to Texas after the war, found nothing left for him there. Eventually enlisted with us."

"You were certain I'd reject him," Falk said.

"Yes, of course."

"I'll take him."

The major nodded to show he was not surprised. He read off another name.

"Private Dunnegan, an Irish immigrant enlistee. A natural fighter. Totally uneducated, but intelligent enough. A willing soldier."

"Taken."

"Private Gruber," the major read. "German extraction. An immigrant, too, in fact. A by-the-book soldier who accepts discipline well. He'll give you no trouble."

Falk said, "I will tolerate no trouble from any of them. But I'll take him, of course."

"You are more easily satisfied than I expected," Forrest said.

"If they are good soldiers, as you have indicated for the most part, I'll whip them into the shape I want them," Falk said.

Forrest frowned. "I've picked them for your acceptance, Captain, because I feel they will perform effectively on the mission you are about to undertake. But it is with some reservation."

"And what's that?"

"That you treat them as men, Captain."

"I have been commanding men as long as you have, Major."

Forrest refrained from making an answering comment to that.

He needed Falk, needed him to end the criticism that was growing against himself. It wouldn't do to antagonize Falk by expressing his dislike of Falk's tyrannical method of command.

"I need one more," Falk said.

"You said six."

"Not another soldier. A scout."

"I have only one. A half-breed Gosiute. And he is almost constantly in use, spying out intentions of the Indians when not guiding us against them. I can't spare him at this time." Forrest paused. "But, as I told you, Private Barlow has a good knowledge of this part of Nevada."

"I guess he'll have to do," Falk said.

On October 1, Captain Falk took to the field with his force.

Major Forrest stood on the porch of his headquarters and watched as they rode out of the fort.

Falk at once ordered Barlow to ride beside him. Barlow, a lean, sinewy trooper with a weathered face, looked nearer to forty than to the thirty that Forrest had said he was.

The squad carried rations for a ten-day patrol, and Falk waited for Barlow to ask their destination.

Instead, Barlow said nothing.

Finally, Falk broke the silence between them.

"We'll be patrolling the area of Pioche, Trooper."

"Yes, sir."

"You are familiar with it?"

"Some, sir. Though most of our actions have taken place not that far south. Schell Creek and the old emigrant and pony express routes from the east where old Fort Schellbourne used to be, that's been sort of our southern limits."

Falk was disappointed. He said angrily, "I was told you knew the terrain."

"As well as anybody on the post, sir. It's just that most of our actions have been north of where I said."

"We are going south," Falk said.

Barlow had been in the army long enough to know an angry officer could mean trouble for an enlisted man, so he said, "Well, I have been to Pioche a time or two. It's just that most of our troubles have been in other directions."

Falk rode in silence with his anger at Forrest's lack of preciseness.

Barlow said, "Might I ask, sir, what is the purpose of this patrol?"

"We are out to put an end to the stage robberies in the vicinity."

"Do you know where the deserters' hideout might be, sir?"

"I do not. I was hoping that you would." The anger rose again in Falk's voice.

"Maybe we can find it, sir."

"By God, maybe we'd better!"

"If I might offer an opinion, sir, they might be holing up sometimes across the Utah border. It isn't far away, you know."

"Of course I know," Falk said. "I've been studying the available maps."

"Yes, sir." After a pause, Barlow said, "If I could see the maps, sir, it might be I could be of more help."

Somewhat grudgingly, Falk took a crude map of the area from a pocket of his blouse and handed it to Barlow.

The enlisted man unfolded and scanned it, then said, "There's a lot of blank spots along the border area."

Falk said irritably, "I know that. And that's where I was led to believe you could fill in."

"I'll do my best, sir."

Barlow led them eastward from the fort, winding up a steep trail into a narrow canyon beside a creek that flowed down from the range of mountains that bordered them on either side.

Two hours' riding took them down the far side to a junction with the north-south road that Falk recognized as the stage route from Wells to Pioche. The canyon trail shortcut saved them forty or fifty miles. Falk began to think that Barlow might well be of use to him.

Once on the stage route, Falk took the lead, setting a pace of alternate walk and trot.

That night they bivouacked near a stage station north of a vast dry alkali flat.

The next day they came to a place along the road that Falk instantly recognized as the location where Madden had held up his stage.

He halted his column.

Barlow gave him a questioning look.

Falk said, "If you were a bandit robbing a stage at this point, and had a hideout across the border in Utah, which way would you go?"

"Why, east, sir."

"Dammit, man! I know that. I want to know if you can pick up trail sign."

"Trail sign?" Barlow said. "You think there was a stage robbed here, sir?"

"I know there was," Falk said. "I was on it."

"Was it the deserters that done it, sir?"

"It was."

"I seldom been easterly of this point," Barlow said. "Not this far south."

"That figures," Falk said testily. "What I'm asking is, are you any good at tracking?"

"Well, sir, I picked up some from that half-breed scout the major keeps around the fort as guide when we go out against the Injuns."

"Let's hope you picked up enough to do us some good," Falk said.

"Yes, sir," Barlow said. "Let's hope that's so."

Falk looked at the rest of the still-mounted squad. Which one was it that Forrest said might be noncom material? Wilkes, that was it.

"Wilkes!"

Wilkes looked up. "Yes, sir!"

"Keep the squad here. Dismount and hold horses. I don't want confusing hoof prints in this area."

"Yes, sir."

"We'll scout for tracks to the east," Falk said to Barlow, and led to a series of sagebrushed knolls in that direction.

Barlow said, "There's been horses ride through here recent, sir."

"*I* can see that," Falk said.

"Leading easterly, too, sir."

Falk didn't bother to comment. The soil here was sandy, and the tracks were plain enough.

"Go bring up the men," Falk said.

"Yes, sir." Barlow turned and rode back.

He soon returned, followed by Wilkes leading the others.

As they came up, Falk rode ahead, following the tracks that wound through the hummocks.

Was it going to be this easy? he thought.

Even as he wondered, they came out of the hillocks and faced a wide desolate expanse of desert that reached to a purplish range of mountains.

Falk halted, unfolded his map, and studied it.

"Snake Range," he said.

"Yes, sir," Barlow said. "I figured so."

Falk did not inquire how he'd figured it. He was sure the man was a liar.

As if he sensed this, Barlow said, "One time we went into them mountains, chasing some Injuns. I recall that now."

"Oh? And did you catch them?"

"No, sir, we didn't."

"Why not?"

"I reckon because they just up and disappeared once they reached them mountains."

"Didn't you have a scout?"

"Oh, yes, sir. That half-breed Gosiute of Major Forrest's."

"And they got away?"

"Yes, sir."

"Poor choice of scouts, I'd say."

Barlow was silent.

"What tribe of Indians were they?" Falk said.

Barlow held his silence a while longer.

"Barlow!"

"Gosiutes, is my belief, sir."

"Your belief? Why?"

"Because of how we seemed to lose the trail when we got in them mountains, sir."

"I don't understand," Falk said.

Again, Barlow was silent.

"Why?" Falk said.

"Well, sir, it has been a peculiar thing, to my way of thinking, but whenever we are chasing Paiutes or Shoshones, we sometimes seem to have better luck than when we're chasing Gosiutes."

"You're implying that they are smarter?"

"They may be, sir." Barlow paused. "But it usually happens when Girard is with us. Girard is the name of the scout, sir."

"You're saying he perhaps leads you deliberately astray?"

"I wouldn't go so far as to say that, sir."

Falk said, "But he is half Gosiute, himself, is that it?"

"Yes, sir. Half Gosiute."

"That's a serious charge, soldier. In view of the fact that Major Forrest seems to think highly of him."

"Begging your pardon, sir, but I ain't making no charge. It's just a thought occurred to me a time or two."

"I see," Falk said. What Barlow had just said interested him.

It could be another example of Forrest's laxness of command. The thought made him feel good.

He was almost cheerful when he spoke again. "Well, Barlow, let's see how much good you can be when we get into those mountains."

CHAPTER 9

AFTER the aborted robbery of his safe, Crowell gave Craig a raise in wages and laudatory thanks.

"You are a good man," he said. "And I'm glad to have you in our employ."

Craig was appreciative of both the raise and the compliment. But, resuming his guard duty, it was only a matter of days before the old boredom once again set in.

A realization came to him now that he could never be satisfied in this type of job.

He had joined the army because he desired action, and he now felt a great loss at being discharged from a career he had liked.

True, there were long, dull periods of garrison life between actions, but there was always the expectant knowledge that more would come.

His life, now, held no such promises. The brief action against the burglars had been a fluke occurrence. And it had all been over in a matter of minutes. A man of action, as he now knew he had the temperament to be, could not long abide the soul-destroying monotony of idleness for hours on end, day after day or night after night.

For a brief moment he even weighed his present existence against Madden's exploits. He had to admit that he'd enjoyed the excitement. It was being an outlaw and the inflicting of harm on innocent men that he could not tolerate.

It had occurred to him that he might have the talents to become a lawman. All he perhaps lacked was experience.

There was law of a sort in Pioche. As the seat of Lincoln County, it housed the sheriff's office, a political appointment that changed almost as frequently as the wind. Deputies were about, but the consensus of the citizens was that all were in the pocket of one or another of the mining companies, and somtimes in the pocket of several.

Therefore, respect for the official law was considerably tainted.

The situation disenchanted him. He would want to be an honest lawman, or not one at all.

He was still pondering this dilemma, doing his monotonous stint, when Crowell called him into his office.

The mine head was not one to waste words.

He said, "I have the feeling, Craig, that you find the job you're doing not much of a challenge. The recent encounter with the safe robbers was an exception, of course. That encounter, in fact, led to the proposition I'm going to offer you."

Craig waited, curious.

"It confirmed what I have believed from the beginning, that you have qualifications that could be put to better use. I have decided to put a company guard on our payroll shipments, in addition to those in the hire of the stage line."

"Wells Fargo has some experienced men," Craig said.

"Granted," Crowell said. "But we have lost two more payrolls to holdups these past weeks, despite their presence. One was to your former army associates. Other mining companies have taken losses, too. That, of course, does not directly concern me." He paused. "But I am the first mine official to decide to use a trusted man of his own." He paused again. "Perhaps others will follow, if my idea proves effective."

"You are offering me the job?" Craig said.

"Yes," Crowell said. "How does it sound to you?"

When Craig did not respond immediately Crowell said, "You are hesitant. I would guess because of the likelihood you may sooner or later have to face your former comrades."

Craig nodded.

"I have laid it out for you, Craig. The job will pay well. It will get you out of the rut of what amounts to dull sentry duty. But it is your choice. I will hold the opening for you for two weeks. After that I will seek someone else."

"Thank you, sir. I will think about it. Very seriously."

"You do that," Crowell said.

Somewhere after the Fort Halleck squad entered the fringe of the Snake Range and the tracks they had been following turned southeasterly, they lost them in an area of limestone.

Hours of spread-out search did not pick them up again.

Falk's suspicion that Barlow was an incompetent guide was reaffirmed, and with it grew his impatience.

Finally, he drew the trooper aside. "I have the feeling you are bluffing."

"Begging your pardon, sir," Barlow said, "But bluffing I am not. It just appears that I'm not good enough."

Falk did not look pleased at the reply. But, after a moment, he said, "The fact remains, we are wasting time. At last sight, the trace was heading to the southeast. Do you have any idea what lies in that direction?"

Barlow hesitated, then said, "No, sir, I don't. After we lost those Gosiutes that time, we turned back."

"Well," Falk said, "*I'm* not turning back. We'll press on the way we've been going."

"Yes, sir," Barlow said.

But very soon they were halted in their course as it ended in a blind canyon. They retraced their steps to where they had entered the foothills.

"We'll skirt the range," Falk said. "If there is a pass through, we've missed it. But, by God, I'm going to see what's on the other side. So we'll keep on, go around the end of it."

"If there is an end, sir."

"From the map, I judge there is, although where is pretty vague. But it seems all the Nevada ranges are relatively short in length, although there are countless numbers of them."

"I can vouch for that, sir," Barlow said.

They rode for miles along a desert fringe, and even now, in October, the clear afternoon sun scorched them.

It put Falk in mind of Fort Maxon and the post command he'd had there. In mind of when he'd sent out lieutenants such as Arnett to lead the patrols.

Well, there'd be another post command for him in the future, he was certain. Perhaps as soon as he ended the criminal activities of the deserters. Not only would this give him an ultimate satisfaction of revenge, it would also look impressive on his service record.

The thought caused him to feel good, despite his physical discomfort. So good that he spoke civilly to the hapless trooper riding at his side.

"Barlow, how's our water holding out?"

"Half canteens, sir."

The good feeling left him.

PART III
Pursuit

CHAPTER 10

CRAIG had decided.

He made his way to the Crowell mine office the morning after a long eventless night shift.

Crowell greeted him with a questioning look.

"I'll take that job, if it's still open," Craig said.

Crowell looked pleased. "I'm glad you accepted. I might have been a little premature, but I made some preliminary arrangements with the stage company, in your behalf. You'll be on my payroll, but you'll ride north as an extra guard for passengers and whatever shipments are going in that direction.

"After receiving our cash payroll at Wells, shipped from Carson City by rail, its protection will be your primary responsibility. You will ride inside the coach both ways. Coming back, you will have the treasure chest under your feet."

"A little unusual, isn't it, sir? Mine company hiring its own guard to ride the stage?"

Crowell shrugged. "As I said last week, since the stage line seems unable to always protect our interests, I'm taking this step in a try to do it ourselves."

"I understand, sir."

There was a brief silence, then Crowell said, "As I mentioned when I first brought this job offer up to you, we have been hit by your former comrades. And it could well happen again, since they have been active against other mine company shipments, as you know."

"Yes, sir."

"I take it then that you've considered this."

"For several days, sir. It is a problem I will just have to face up to, if it happens."

"I'm glad you understand that," Crowell said. "This could be the beginning of a career for you, Craig. One in which your army background can be put to good use. This, despite your unfortunate discharge."

"That was my thinking, too, sir."

Crowell smiled. "Hard to break the habit, isn't it?"

"Habit, sir?"

"Your habit of 'sirring' others."

"Yes, sir. If they're in a position of authority, it is."

"You'll adjust to civilian life after a while."

"I hope so," Craig said. "Sir."

Craig made his first run north without event. On the return trip, with the payroll chest at his feet, he rode tensely alert. There were only two passengers, men who looked like miners, who told him they had come from the fading mining district at Bruno City, up near the Idaho border.

Craig did not wholly believe them, and although neither appeared to be armed, he frequently glanced at them, often to find them staring back.

At such moments he came close to regretting that he'd taken on the new job.

After several miles, one of them said, "Been riding guard for Wells Fargo long?"

Craig saw no reason to clarify who his employer was. He said, "Why do you ask?"

The passenger said, "Mostly they carry shotguns."

"Sometimes there are exceptions," Craig said, meeting the man's eyes and holding there.

After a moment, the man dropped his eyes and said, "Sure, sure, I reckon that's so."

Craig felt like pushing it a little, and he said. "Some of us are more handy with a six-gun. Know what I mean?"

"Sure, sure," the passenger said. "I didn't mean no offense. Just making conversation, is all."

"No offense taken," Craig said, and let it go at that.

But he noticed that from then on both men seemed a little uneasy.

Craig decided to play on their uneasiness. He drew his gun, turned the cylinder as if checking the loads, then put the weapon back in his holster.

"You expecting trouble?" the other passenger said.

"I always expect it," Craig said. "So I'm always ready."

"I see," the man said.

Craig, searching his face, thought he looked worried.

"Sure hope there ain't none while I'm aboard," the man said. "Them bullets get to flying around, somebody can get hurt."

"That's a fact to remember," Craig said.

He was a little surprised when the stage eventually pulled safely into Pioche.

The two passengers bid him good-bye, seemingly as relieved as he was.

Crowell was waiting with an armed escort to take the chest to his headquarters, from where the miners were paid.

As the passengers left, Craig's relief was mixed with a measure of self-criticism at his unwarranted fears.

It shows how a man's imagination can sometimes get the best of him, he thought. Well, he was new at this game. He was sure he would become more confident with experience.

Yet, a bit of doubt remained with him that his companions on the ride might not have been innocent.

Could it be that his own aggressive front had forestalled a robbery attempt on their part? He guessed he'd never know for sure.

He supposed such doubts were a part of the job. It was something he'd have to learn to live with.

As it was, he felt let down when Crowell welcomed his arrival.

When Craig joined the escort taking the money to the mine, Crowell said, "It appears you brought us luck this shipment."

"If so," Craig said, "that's all I did."

"It's enough, Craig. But don't think it will always be so. You'll be earning your pay the hard way some of these times."

"I suppose," Craig said.

"I'm glad it didn't happen on your first run, though."

"To be truthful, sir, so am I."

Crowell turned to give him an appraising look. He smiled slightly and said, "Truthful, you are. You're still young enough to be honest. But soon you'll learn to bluff and brass in order to contend with those around you who do the same. In this mining business, Craig, few of us are wholly honest. It's a matter of survival in a rough game. Do not expect too much from anybody."

Craig, a little surprised by the words, took them in silence, weighing them.

"And stop addressing me as sir," Crowell said. "You're not in the army now. You understand what I'm saying?"

"I think so, sir," Craig said.

The driver on the next northbound run was the one who had been present at the August shooting by the deserters that had killed the two guards.

Driver Dan Dudley had recovered from his serious wound.

As Craig reported for the run, he felt Dudley's sharp appraisal. Recognizing the jehu, Craig began to sweat.

Did the man sense something familiar about him, even though he had only seen Craig with his face hidden?

Finally, Dudley said, "So you're the gunhand that Crowell hired to ride inside the coach."

Craig nodded.

"Last run I drove," the oldster said, "the inside guard got hisself killed."

"I heard," Craig said.

"Let's hope you have better luck."

"I figure on it," Craig said.

"Way I heard, Crowell hired you on account you killed a couple burglars was robbing his safe."

"I was doing a job he was paying me to do," Craig said.

"Looks like you got the right attitude, then," Dudley said.

Craig felt a quick relief.

"Though damned if there don't seem to be something familiar about you. Something I can't rightly put my finger on."

Craig's relief left him. He said, "Must have seen me around the town, I expect."

"I reckon that must be it," Dudley said.

The stage shotgun guard came up, and Dudley said, "Craig, you know Rich Jones?"

Jones, a solidly built man of forty, in a soiled gray suit, spoke up. "We been on a previous run together. Nothing happened. He may be good luck."

"Glad to hear that," the jehu said. "It's got so we live on luck in this business."

"Ain't that the truth?" Jones said.

"All right," Dudley said. "Let's get on our way."

He climbed up on the box, followed by Jones. Craig got in the coach. There appeared to be no passengers leaving Pioche on this run.

The trip north was damn near as boring as guarding the mine, Craig thought. And a hell of a lot more uncomfortable.

But eventually the stage reached Wells.

The payroll chest was taken from the rail express car and loaded into the coach, and the relief driver who had taken over on the northern stretch started his team on the southbound run, again without passengers.

The long ride began again, the stage stopping every twelve to fifteen miles at crude swing stations for a change of horses. There a couple of stock handlers would rush out from a clutch of roughly constructed stables and a granary. Within a quarter hour they would have a fresh team in harness and the stage would again be on its way.

Drivers and shotgun guards changed midway at a home station, to sleep and await their next stint when the stage returned from Wells. But, as the Crowell guard, Craig had had to catch whatever sleep he could in the continuing stage's onward journey to Wells and immediate return. It took some getting used to, as the coach rocked and swayed and jolted along on its thoroughbraces.

At the change station, Dudley once more took over the reins, and Jones replaced the relief shotgun on the box.

"No trouble, eh?" Jones said to Craig.

"None, so far," Craig said.

"Well, you're halfway home," Jones said, climbing up beside the driver.

"Yeah." Craig got into the coach.

"Let's go!" Dudley shouted, and got the team moving.

The miles went by. Craig, alone inside the stage, dozed. Several swing stops later they reached Conner's Station, where a road went west toward Hamilton and the White Pine mining district.

They grabbed a twenty-minute meal there and were on their way south again.

Craig awoke from a doze to hear Dudley cussing above even the noise of the team and coach. The first words he made out sounded like a loud argument between Dudley and the shotgun guard.

"You going to stop?" Jones said. "There's a half a dozen of them sonsabitches."

"Hell, no, I ain't!" the driver said.

"You can't outrun them."

"You don't know that. Them sonsabitches must have rid in from their hideout. If so, they got tired horses. And we got a fresh team at Conner's."

"You're taking a hell of a chance," Jones said. "From what I can see, it looks like that deserter bunch."

"I stopped for them last time," the jehu said. "And the bastards shot me anyways!"

"I don't like it," the shotgun guard said.

"The hell with you," Dudley said, and the coach lurched forward as Dudley put the team into a run.

Craig could no longer hear voices from the box.

What he heard was the sound of shots. He chanced sticking his head out to look back, and he saw Madden's bunch coming onto the road and taking up the chase.

It appeared the old man had surprised them in making a run for it, and he had gained a couple of hundred yards' lead.

There was no firing from the pursuers now. They were seasoned men who knew the futility of shooting revolvers at that distance from horseback.

As he watched, Craig began to think old Dudley might have made the right decision. It appeared the deserters' mounts had already put some distance on them; they were now barely holding even with the coach's pace.

He was hoping it was so.

Because if they caught the coach, he'd have to face up to a shoot-out with them. Once his comrades. He felt a sickening dread.

A mile went by, and they had not gained, and Craig's hopes rose.

Suddenly the road curved, shutting off his view except for one rider who had pulled ahead of the others, and he guessed it could be Madden himself. The rider drew his carbine, raised it for high trajectory, and fired a wild shot.

Foolish, Craig thought. And then, a moment later, he was not so sure.

The stage began to slow. It faltered erratically. Dudley was having trouble with his team.

Craig leaned out of the cab to look forward, and he could

see a mist of blood spurting from the neck of the near lead horse. It appeared to stumble, regained its footing, then stumbled again, veering the team toward its side.

Craig felt Dudley reining in, heard him curse savagely as he pulled the stage to a halt. And at that moment the wounded horse went down to its knees.

Stopped just in time, Craig thought, to avoid a pile-up of horseflesh, stage, and men.

But just in time for what else?

Because now he could hear the riders pounding toward them.

He threw a glance backward, and drew his gun.

The showdown had come.

As the deserter troop rode up, Dudley, still seated on the box, called down to Craig, "For God's sake, hold your fire! This ain't no time for heroics."

"I've got a chest down here to protect," Craig called back.

"We made our try!" the driver yelled. "Don't be a damn fool! You'll get us all killed."

He is right, Craig thought. In a running fight they might have had a chance. They had lost that chance when the fluke carbine shot struck the horse.

Now, held immobile by the horse slowly dying in the harness, with the squad of ex-cavalry closing in, it would be suicide to open fire.

They came in, each holding a revolver ready to blast.

He could identify each one easily, by build, saddle posture, and horse, despite the neckerchief masks.

Madden and his six, still intact. It was obvious they had not yet suffered a serious casualty during their life of crime.

He wondered if they had killed any more of their victims.

And he wondered what their reaction to his presence would be. He would soon know, he thought grimly.

He holstered his gun, not liking himself for doing so, but knowing it was the sensible thing to do. He sat back inside the coach, shadowed in its dimness against the outside glare of the sun.

He heard Madden's voice as he called to the shotgun guard, "Put that damn Greener down!"

Jones must have lowered the shotgun, because Madden then addressed Dudley. "Well, old man, I see you healed up all right."

"No thanks to you," Dudley said shortly.

"Now, that's no way to talk. We let you go that other time, didn't we?"

Dudley didn't answer.

"Didn't we?"

"All right, goddammit, yes!" the driver said.

"Glad to see you appreciate it," Madden said.

Slack's voice spoke out then. "Let me shoot the old son of a bitch."

Craig thought, That's Slack, and that's what he said that other time.

The driver must have remembered, too, because he said, "Still got that trigger-happy one with you, eh?"

Slack said, "And still ready to pull that trigger, old man. You best mind your manners."

Dudley must have realized that Slack was serious, because he said, "I didn't mean no offense, mister. It's just that sometimes I got a big mouth."

Madden said, "It's payroll time, men. Take a look in the coach there."

Slack and one other dismounted, moved to the coach door, and threw it open.

Slack and Craig stared at each other.

Madden had ridden over and taken the shotgun lying at Jones's feet. Now he moved off a bit and said, "Is it in there?"

"What you mean by *it*?" Slack said.

"The payroll chest, what else?"

"Yeah, it's here," Slack said. "But we got another *it* in here, too." He backed away from the coach door. "Get the hell out of there," he said to Craig.

Craig stepped out and stood in the roadway, looking up at Madden.

Madden stared, then his eyes dropped to Craig's gun, went back to his face. "You a passenger or riding guard, Craig?"

"Riding guard."

"Sorry to hear that," Madden said. "That puts us on opposite sides."

"Looks like it does."

"Surprises me, you taking a job like that," Madden said. "Didn't you know you'd likely run up against us?"

"It occurred to me," Craig said.

"And you decided to do it anyway?"

"I'm here."

Slack said then, "It don't look like you're doing much of a job of it."

Craig was silent.

Madden's voice was suddenly hard, harder than it had ever been with Craig. He said, "I offered you every chance, Raymond. I wanted you with us."

Craig held his silence.

"I can't have you against us," Madden said.

Craig flicked a glance at Slack, and saw Slack's hard readiness to act as executioner.

Would Madden give the word?

Before Madden could say anything Craig saw the quick gleam in Slack's eyes, the desire to kill, and the twitch of his hand darting for his gun.

Instinctively, Craig grabbed for his own.

Slack's bullet drove him backward into the coach.

Dudley and Jones had climbed down from the box and stood watching. It was too much for Jones, who had a gun hidden in a shoulder holster. He pulled the gun and fired at Slack.

And missed.

The ex-troopers opened fire on him and the driver, riddling them with bullets.

Madden cursed, then turned his attention back to Craig, now sprawled unconscious over the payroll chest on the coach floor.

"Ease him out," he said.

Slack reached for Craig's feet and began to tug.

"Not you, goddammit," Madden said. "Stand away!"

Slack backed off and said, "You saw him grab for his gun, Sarge."

"Get away from him," Madden said. "I saw no such thing."

"Well, he did," Slack said.

Madden began to pull gently, holding to Craig's ankles, and got him partly out of the cab. There was blood welling from Craig's shoulder.

"We've got to stop that blood," Madden said.

One of the deserters, standing behind him, said, "We ain't got time for that, Sarge."

"The hell we haven't," Madden said, leaning over to open Craig's coat.

"Look up the road," the man said. "There's three riders coming."

Hiller said, "Sarge, they catch us red-handed we'll have to kill them too."

"Grab that chest and let's ride," Parrett said. "We done too much killing already."

Madden seemed not to hear. He said again, "We've got to stop that bleeding."

"We got to ride," Parrett said. "Them riders coming can tend to Craig. That's better than more killing."

Madden finally seemed to listen. He withdrew from the coach doorway and looked up the road at the approaching men.

"All right," he said, after a moment. He gestured toward one of the mounted ex-troopers. "Lift the chest up to where he can carry it a ways across his pommel. We'll open it after we get clear."

One of the dismounted men did so.

Madden turned back to Craig, and even though he could see that Craig was unconscious, he said, "Raymond, there's men coming that can tend to you. We got to ride."

"He don't hear you, Sarge," Slack said. "Can't you see that?"

Madden looked at him with hard eyes. "Shut up!" he said.

They all got mounted then, with Hiller balancing the chest awkwardly over his saddle, and rode off to the east.

From a half mile away, Madden took a last look back to see the riders on the road reach the stalled coach with its downed horse, dead driver and shotgun messenger, and a wounded, bleeding unconscious Craig.

He swore long and loud.

Then, before he turned back to the trail, he spoke, as if addressing the distant horsemen. "Stop that bleeding first thing. And take care of him, you understand?"

The three riders were dressed as buckaroos, probably from a cattle ranch over in Spring Valley.

"Christ!" one of them said. "What have we here?"

"That bunch we saw ride away," one of the others said. "Like I thought, it was a holdup."

They stared at the two bodies lying in the dust of the road.

"Holdup?" the third one said. "It looks more like a damn massacre."

"A true fact for sure," the first one said.

At that moment they heard the groan from within the coach, and looked toward where Craig's form could be seen lying on the floor where Madden had carefully laid him.

"There's one that ain't dead!"

The first one swung down and stepped quickly toward the stage.

He looked in, stared at the blood-soaked neckerchief Madden had stuffed against the wound.

"Somebody tried to help him," he said, "before they rode off."

One peered over his shoulder. "That bandanna—it's yellow like them cavalry bandits been wearing."

"Reckon we know who done this then," the other said. "Give me a hand here. We got to tie that wad of cloth tighter to keep him from bleeding to death."

"I'll rip a shirt off one them dead fellers," the third buckaroo said. "They sure as hell ain't needing them no more."

"Get at it then."

With a shirt ripped into strips, the other two got the compress fastened tight enough to stanch the blood flow.

"Must have pulled his gun on them bandits," the third man said. "There it is, lying on the floor."

"Stage was headed for Pioche, I reckon."

"What we got to do is cut that downed horse out of the traces, load them bodies on, and take the coach on in. This one with the wound has got a chance maybe, we get him to a doctor."

The remaining horses were skittish from the smell of blood, and it took all the skill of the buckaroos to control them while they got the task done.

They rearranged the harness, and one took the reins and moved the team away from the dying animal. One of the men ended its suffering with a close shot behind its ear.

They then tied their mounts behind the coach, and one took the box beside the driver, while the other got in the cab to keep a vigil on the wounded man.

"Handling a stage team like this ain't my specialty," the man holding the reins said.

"All you got to do is keep them moving along," the buckaroo beside him said. "Them horses most likely know the way."

CHAPTER 11

JOHN Crowell said, "How is he?"

Crowell was standing in the office of Hiram Faraday, the doctor that he and his company used for all emergencies.

Faraday looked up from his examination of Craig's wound, now three days old.

"A close call," the doctor said. "Those three buckaroos saved his life by getting the stage in when they did."

"The wound is that bad?"

"No, not the wound itself, the loss of blood and the shock that loss caused. The wound was clean, the bullet went through. Tore a lot of tissue but missed both bone and muscle. He'll be suffering soreness for some time, but he'll be back on the job in a few more days."

"Back on the job," Crowell said. He gave Craig, who was sitting in the doctor's examination chair, a weighing look. "Are you ready for that, Craig?"

Craig met his glance. He did not speak at once, then he said, "No, I don't think so."

Crowell looked thoughtful, then nodded. "Your old comrades came close to killing you. That's bound to make you think twice."

"That's true," Craig said.

"I understand," Crowell said. "You can have your old job back. It's a lot less risky."

"No," Craig said, "you don't quite understand. Being shot down by them made me do some heavy thinking, but not the way you believe."

"What do you mean?"

"It made me think that simply trying to guard the shipments is not the way to handle this. Not against a seven-man force of criminals."

"What else can we do?"

"I hate to admit it, but that sonofabitching Captain Falk was right about hunting them down."

Crowell thought about this, then said, "Falk reported in at Fort Halleck some time ago, I heard. Rumor has it he's been out with a detail, searching for them, several times. Without success, obviously."

"Because he doesn't know their habits," Craig said. "He doesn't know their hideout. He doesn't know the trails they follow to and from their attacks. I do."

"You refused his request to hire on as scout for his detail," Crowell said.

"You know I hate him," Craig said. "And you know why."

"Yes."

"And that's something that will never change."

"I understand," Crowell said.

"And you know how I felt about Madden and the others. Old comrades, and all."

"I do." Crowell was staring at him now.

Craig stared back. "That's what changed. They shot me," Craig said. "And they killed old Dudley and Rich Jones."

"Yes."

"That's what caused the change," Craig said.

Crowell's face reflected thought. He said, "You'll volunteer now to scout for Falk?"

"The killings will go on," Craig said, "and Falk is the only hope of stopping them. I can see that now."

Crowell took this statement in silence. Finally he nodded. "I think you're right."

Craig turned to Faraday. "Doc, when can I ride?"

"A week, maybe. But you'll be hurting for some time to come."

"A week till I can ride," Craig said. "But I can take the stage north to get to Fort Halleck now."

Crowell's eyes were on him again. He said, "Craig, are you sure you can do this?"

"I'm well enough to ride the stage."

"I don't mean that. I mean can you go against your one-time friends?"

"I feel I have to," Craig said. "I see no other way."

He took the stage north, this time as a passenger at Crowell's expense. Crowell had also given him ample fare to ride the Central Pacific from Wells to Halleck Station.

At the station he lucked out, catching a freight wagon bound for the post.

The teamster was a willing talker as he drove.

After covertly eyeing Craig a couple of times, he said, "You a new recruit for the major?"

"No," Craig said. "Why do you ask?"

"Just curious," the teamster said. "You got kind of a trooper look about you. And the major, he sure as hell could use more help."

"How come?"

"Ain't you heard? I mean, about the damn Injuns raising more and more hell here and there around the district?"

"I've been down Pioche way," Craig said.

"Ain't been no trouble down there?" the teamster said. "Injun trouble, I mean?"

"None I heard about."

"Well, up this way they been having more than usual, it seems. Kind of like them redskins is leading up to something big. And it seems to be getting worse."

"Sorry to hear that," Craig said.

"Ain't we all? For quite a spell the Injuns wasn't much trouble, but now they got some rabble-rousing Injun calls hisself Chief Lone Horse stirring them up and keeping Forrest's troopers busy."

Craig said, "I guess that's why they can't get the army to stop the stage robberies down south."

"You mean by them the newspapers call the deserter troop?"

"Yeah."

"It has been the reason, I expect," the teamster said. "But I heard now they got a new officer at the post to take a patrol after them."

"He having any luck?"

"Not that I've heard of."

The teamster was silent for a spell, then he said, "I hate a goddam Injun worse than poison!"

"How come?"

"They make me nervous, way they been acting up. Hell, I keep expecting them to attack me for the supplies I'm hauling."

"I guess that would make a man nervous," Craig said.

"You're damn right it does."

The miles went slow, but eventually they drove into the fort.

The teamster pulled up next to the commissary. He looked curiously at Craig. Craig throughout the trip had not revealed his reason for being there. The teamster felt a little put out about that.

Now, he said, "Yonder along the parade ground is the headquarters."

"So I see," Craig said, giving him a little more to think about.

"You say you never been a soldier?" the teamster said.

"No, I never said that," Craig said. "Thanks for the ride."

He walked along the edge of the parade toward the headquarters.

Inside, an orderly looked up from a battered desk.

"I'm looking for a Captain Falk," Craig said.

"He's out on a patrol," the corporal said.

"When will he be back?"

"Couldn't say. Been gone three, four days. May be out the rest of the week."

"Major Forrest, then."

"What about?"

Craig hesitated. He had once been under the command of the major, before Falk had taken over the post at Maxon. He remembered Forrest as a fair and able officer, and he supposed the major would remember him.

"About a job as scout for Captain Falk's detachment," Craig said.

"A scout? You familiar with this area?"

"Just give the major my request."

The orderly frowned, and gave him a long look. "Your name?"

"Ex-Private Raymond Craig."

The corporal got up and went to the major's door, opened it, and went in.

Craig heard the murmur of his voice. There was a short silence, then he heard the major say, "Send him in."

The orderly came out and jerked his thumb toward the office.

Craig nodded and moved toward it.

Inside, he stopped and stood at attention.

Forrest looked at him with an unreadable face. "Ex-Private Craig," he said.

"Yes, sir."

"It has been a while, Craig."

"It has, sir."

"What can I do for you?"

"It's like I told the corporal, sir. About scouting for Captain Falk's detachment. I understand Captain Falk now has a detail out trying to put an end to the stage attacks by First Sergeant Madden," Craig said.

"*Ex*–First Sergeant Madden," the major said. "Yes, that's true."

"I've heard he has not been successful."

"As yet, no."

"That's where I believe I can be of help to him," Craig said.

"Help to him? You?"

"Yes, sir. In fact, several weeks ago, he contacted me in Pioche and suggested the same. At that time, I refused."

"And now?"

"I've changed my mind, sir."

"Why?"

"Two reasons, sir. One, they have become killers. They have killed several guards. And, most recently, they killed a driver. Two, they shot me as I was riding as a mine company guard, and left me to die."

"Brought it home to you personally, did they?"

"Yes, sir."

"That would make a difference, I suppose," the major said. He paused. "Falk told me the background of all this. His version, of course. But from what he said, you rode up from Arizona with this bunch after they deserted his command. Is that correct?"

"Yes, sir, it is."

"But you later left them? Why?"

"I'm not cut out for the kind of life they're leading," Craig said.

"I see." The major looked thoughtful. Finally, he said, "I recall you as a good soldier, Craig. I do not understand the details that caused your court-martial and its verdict. But I believe it probable that you have a powerful resentment against Captain Falk. A grudge that could lead, conceivably, to violence against him."

Craig made no comment.

"So I will not decide this issue at this time. Captain Falk and his patrol went out with rations for five days. They have been gone three. It will be his decision to make when he returns.

"Meanwhile, you will stay here, take your meals at the company mess, and bunk in the quarters of our half-breed scout. I'll have an extra cot moved in there for you. Will that be satisfactory?"

"Yes, sir. Thank you, sir." Craig said, and caught himself just as he began to salute. He turned quickly then and left the office.

Major Forrest looked after him, thinking about the aborted salute. Too bad what happened to him, he thought. Whatever the reason, Craig had had the makings of a top soldier.

It was too late now to help him, but the major made a mental note to learn more about the court-martial.

Near noon, two days later, Craig looked across the fort's compound and saw Falk lead his patrol into the parade ground, swinging their tired mounts into a line.

The shoulders of the troopers sagged with fatigue. Only Falk sat erect in his saddle, his voice arrogant as ever as he dismissed the detail.

He dismounted then, handed his horse to an orderly, and strode directly toward the headquarters structure while the troopers rode off toward the stables.

Forrest waited for him on the porch.

As Falk stepped up, the major said, "Any luck?"

"None."

Forrest led the way into his office, motioned to a chair, and seated himself at his desk. He said, "This was your third patrol so far, and still no luck, eh? Let's have your report."

"Not much to report," Falk said, keeping a matter-of-fact tone. "We scoured a number of trails intersecting the stage routes and leading toward the Utah border. Eventually we lost them in one or another of the mountain ranges."

"And why did you lose them?"

Falk did not answer at once.

"Why, Falk?"

"I'm not familiar with the country," Falk said then. "You know that."

"But Private Barlow is."

"Only to a limited extent," Falk said. "Major, what I need is the loan of that half-breed scout of yours."

"He's with a detachment north of Wells, trying to run down some renegades who attacked a ranch up here and killed the family."

"When do you expect him back?"

The major shrugged. "I can't say. Lieutenant Todd is in command of the detail, with orders to persevere in running the murderers down, as long as there appears to be any hope."

"Major, I need somebody who can lead me to Madden and his desperados. I will solve this problem of the robberies for you then. With dispatch, believe me! But I can't do it with a bumbler like Barlow as a guide."

"Raymond Craig rode in a couple of days ago to offer his services in hunting down your quarry."

"But I tried to hire him weeks ago, in Pioche! He refused."

Forrest said, "Certain events have apparently changed his mind. For one thing, he was shot down by his former comrades while riding as guard on a mine payroll shipment."

"Can you put him on as scout?"

"I can. Can you work with him, that's the question."

"Yes. If he can lead me to Madden's hideout, I will make allowance for his earlier mistakes."

Forrest got up and went to the door and spoke to his orderly. "Have the civilian staying in Girard's quarters report here at once."

"Yes, sir," the orderly said.

Forrest went back to his desk.

He looked again at Falk, and said, "This must come hard to you. I mean your agreeing to utilize the help of a man whose army career you destroyed."

For a moment, Falk seemed to bridle, as if he were about to protest the major's choice of words. Then he got control of himself and said, "I will do whatever I have to do to destroy Madden and his rogues."

The orderly reappeared at the office door. "The civilian is here, sir."

"Send him in," Forrest said.

Craig entered. He ignored Falk, and said, "Major?"

"I've told Falk of your offer to act as guide on the detail that he is undertaking," Forrest said. "I trust your offer still holds?"

"Yes, sir, it does."

"You will be put on civilian scout's pay until his mission is accomplished. With the proviso, of course, that you will be able to work together."

"I understand, sir."

Forrest turned to Falk. "Captain?"

"Agreed," Falk said. But he did not so much as glance at Craig.

Four days later, Falk formed up his detail on the parade, shortly after morning mess.

Major Forrest stood watching in front of headquarters, paying particular attention to the figure of Craig. Once again he wondered what was going through the ex-private's mind. What could he be feeling, setting out to lead an officer he hated against the men who had been his comrades?

He tried to imagine himself in Craig's position, then shook his head.

He was glad, for that moment, that he could not.

Falk's sharp voice intruded on this thought.

"Prepare to mount. Mount!"

There was the slap of thighs against saddles, and the clank of carbines and canteens.

"Right by column of twos, march!"

Captain Falk, with Craig at his left, led the detail across the parade ground, heading south once more. Major Forrest watched until they disappeared beyond the structures on the other side.

Eight hours of riding took them forty miles down the main route to where they reached, near sundown, a stage swing station that was sixty miles south of Wells.

Throughout the day there had been no talk between Falk and Craig. Each seemed to know there was no real need to speak until they neared Madden's theater of depredations, and neither apparently felt any desire to break the strained silence between them until absolutely necessary.

They made camp that night close to the station.

And now Craig grew aware that the troopers from Halleck were curious about his presence with them.

It was to be expected, he thought. They had made at least three futile attempts to hunt down their quarry. And now they were wondering why the addition of a civilian to the squad would make them any more successful.

Word was among them that he was a scout, to take over where Barlow had failed, but Barlow, when questioned, could tell them only that he was their new guide. Beyond that, Barlow had no knowledge.

Tired as they were from the long, hard aimless rides on which Barlow had led them, they were glad of any change. If worthwhile. Still, the curiosity was there, strong enough that Craig could feel it.

It bothered him, because he was vulnerable to Falk's degree of discretion in what he revealed. Craig had no desire to be riding with a squad of troopers who might be informed by Falk that their guide had been drummed out of the service.

He was hoping that Falk's desire to accomplish his mission would preclude any such disclosure. But with the bad blood between them, he could not be certain.

It was Barlow whose curiosity was understandably the greatest. And once the camp was made, and a supper eaten of coffee, hardtack, and bacon, the former guide came over to where Craig lounged apart from the others, as well as from Falk.

"I understand," Barlow said, "that you're the one is going to lead us, at long last, to them deserters been raising hell with the stage shipments."

"I hope to," Craig said.

"I hope so, too," Barlow said. "But the men been asking what be your qualifications for doing so. You understand, I ain't meaning no offense in mentioning this."

Craig had been dreading such an inquiry, and now he said, "I'm not free to tell you that at this time."

Barlow took that in silence, as if he had expected a better answer. He glanced over to where Captain Falk was lounging, also apart from the men, then said, "Captain's orders, maybe?"

When Craig made no reply, he said, "A hard-ass officer, the captain is. Or maybe you know that from experience?"

"Yes," Craig said. "I know."

Barlow nodded. "We been thinking maybe it was so. Been a trooper, your own self, no doubt. Can tell the way you sit that saddle."

Craig again was silent.

"Captain come to us by way of Arizona," Barlow said. "You too?"

The man's probing irritated Craig, but he said, "Yeah."

Barlow was studying him closer now, and said, "The way I hear it, they think that robber bunch we're after, they come from down that way, too."

"That so?" Craig said.

"Been writ up in some the newspapers that they thought they was."

"Big place, Arizona," Craig said.

"Reckon so," Barlow said. "Heard them deserters was from a small post called Fort Maxon."

"That right?"

"Heard the captain, he was from there, too."

"Coincidences happen," Craig said.

"Coincidence? Not the way I heard it. I heard the captain's got a personal grudge against them, account they run off from the post which he had command."

"Be enough to make most any commanding officer mad, wouldn't it?" Craig said.

Barlow's inquisitive eyes were still on him. But all he said was "I reckon so."

CHAPTER 12

THE next day they came to a place where Falk, addressing Craig out of necessity, his tone heavy with his reluctance, said, "On my way to Fort Halleck, the stage was stopped here by Madden. He left tracks going eastward, but Barlow lost them in the mountains."

Craig said nothing.

"Well," Falk said sharply, "does that interest you or not?"

"No," Craig said. "It only indicates that at the time they were still using the hideout."

"Can you find it from here?"

"Maybe I could," Craig said. "But I'm familiar with a trail off the route further south. Closer to Conner's Station."

"So!" Falk said. "You could have saved the army a lot of trouble by letting us know this when I first interrogated you in Pioche."

"Interrogated, Captain? The way I remember it, you damn right pleaded for my help."

Falk scowled. "Pleaded? I plead with no man, Private. I offered you a job."

Craig was silent again.

"A job that you now came seeking." Falk said.

That was true, Craig had to admit. He said, "If our search is going to be successful, we've got to work together. But I'll remind you that you put me out of the army, and so you have no right to address me as Private."

Falk glared at him.

"The name is Craig," Craig said.

"Touchy, aren't you?"

"About being wrongfully driven out of the cavalry? Yes, I guess I am."

Falk did not comment again, and they rode in silence the remainder of that day.

It was dusk when they reached Conner's Station.

They bivouacked there.

In the morning, Craig took to a prospecting trace that led to the east across a broad valley of sage and bunchgrass. To the south of the valley a towering peak rose, dwarfing those of the eastward range.

Barlow, who had ridden up beside Craig and Falk, said, "That's still part of the Snake Range, Captain. Up ahead, I mean. And that big mountain to our right, that's called Wheeler Peak."

Falk said, "If you know this trail, why didn't you lead us to it before?"

"No, sir, I ain't familiar with this trail. I just know the name of that high peak to the south there from having once had it pointed out to me."

"That's a piece of useless information," Falk said. "Drop back into the column. It appears Craig here has knowledge of the terrain."

Rebuffed, Barlow said, "Yes, sir," and returned to his place.

Partway across the valley the trail veered northerly.

"What now?" Falk said.

"There's a high pass through the range up ahead," Craig said. "It can't be seen from here because it cuts back sharp-like. About ten miles ahead the trail turns into it."

"Sounds like you must have ridden it several times," Falk said. "How many robberies did *you* have a hand in?"

"I took no money," Craig said. "I left the bunch when I realized what was going on."

"Indeed?" Falk said. "And how many crimes did it take before you were aware?"

"I'm here now," Craig said, "trying to make amends for

any wrong I have done." He paused. "But I wouldn't expect you to accept that."

"We'll see," Falk said. "We'll see how successful your efforts turn out."

Yes, Craig thought. We'll see, one way or another. But either way, I don't like what I'm doing.

They pushed on, and the trace turned as Craig had described, and brought them to a rising floor of a canyon that rose toward the pass.

As they ascended, the flanks became mantled with pines.

Coming down the other side, they could see before them hills covered with juniper and sage.

As dusk fell east of the Snake Range they reached a mound of rocks piled beside the trail.

Craig said to Falk. "That marks the Utah line."

"Who took the trouble to build the marker?"

"People who need to know which side of the boundary they're on."

"Border jumpers?" Falk said.

Craig nodded. "Rustlers, mostly. Just ahead a couple of miles is a place called Garrison. Cattle stolen in Utah are held there temporarily, eventually driven to markets in the mining districts. There's a stream by the settlement, and enough water to harvest hay. Corrals have been built over the years."

"That's where Madden is?" Falk's excitement showed.

"No, but it's a stopover for him sometimes. He wanted to make it his base, but the rustlers didn't want his company. Him robbing mine payrolls, and them selling beef to the mine people, it just didn't mix."

Falk said, "So Madden let them bluff him."

"No bluff about it," Craig said. "He realized he was out-numbered and out-gunned." He paused. "We can water the horses here and fill the canteens, but that's all. We can camp nearby, and tomorrow we'll have a half-day ride to the hideout." He paused again. "But I'm not sure how they'll take to a squad of cavalry riding in on them."

At Chisco Springs, Madden had turned irascible with his men.

The robbery had been a success, the chest containing pay for the weekly hire of over a hundred Crowell employees.

He should have been satisfied with the way things had worked out.

But he wasn't.

What spoiled his satisfaction was the matter of Raymond Craig being shot by Slack, and perhaps dying. Or, if Craig recovered, would he turn against them?

If so, Madden could blame Slack as being the cause of most of the trouble.

And Slack added to his ire by bringing it all to his mind again by saying, "Sarge, we can't trust Craig no more."

"Your fault," Madden said. "You're the one that shot him."

"Hell, he was grabbing for his gun. It was him or me."

"I don't believe that," Madden said.

"You making me out a liar?"

Some of the others were listening, and Hiller spoke up, "He's maybe right, Sarge. About what Craig might do, I mean."

"What are you saying?" Madden said, although he already knew the answer.

"He could give away where we hole up," Hiller said.

"Which is what I'm getting at," Slack said.

Madden thought about it, scowling, then shrugged. "So they learn our hideout. Who would they send after us?"

Hiller said, "You forgetting Captain Falk was on that other stage we stopped? Didn't he say he was transferred to Fort Halleck?"

Madden was silent, as Hiller's words aroused his own concern that Falk's posting to the fort could have a special link to their attacks on the stage lines.

Recalling his words with Falk at the stage halt earlier, he remembered them as an implied threat. Was Falk sent to track down the deserter troop? Falk's orders had posted him for *detached* duty at the fort. Certainty struck Madden now that his concern had been valid.

Falk would be out to run him down.

And mightn't Craig be the one to guide him?

Of that, he was still not so sure. His uncertainty aroused his anger, and he said, "Goddamn you, Slack, for shooting Ray!"

Slack's face got hard. "Don't be cussing me out, Madden! Ain't none of us in the frigging army no more."

"You're still taking orders from me!" Madden said.

"Orders is one thing," Slack said. "A cussing is something else."

Craig led Falk and his squad around a hillock and there, just ahead, was the jumble of rustlers' shacks. There was also a windmill to pump water from a nearby stream.

In a large corral were penned a couple of dozen cattle.

Seeing that, Craig said, "Fresh stolen, probably. They won't be held long."

"Stolen from where?" Falk said.

"Likely from over Milford way, and headed for the mines of eastern Nevada."

"How many cattle thieves living there?"

"It varies, I'd guess. Most I ever saw was maybe a dozen. They come and go. Been doing so for near twenty years, what I been told."

"They might outnumber us two to one, then."

"Might well be," Craig said. "Best tell the men to keep their hands off their carbines and their fingers away from their holsters. I'll go in holding my palm up in a peace sign. Then it'll be up to you to explain we're not here to bother them. But you better get the message across quick."

"Outlaws," Falk said. "If I had another squad with me, I'd wipe them out."

"Well, Captain, you don't, and you'd best not forget it. The men hanging out here are all hardcases, make no mistake about that." Craig paused. "They'll be wondering why we're here. Best tell them you're after Injuns."

"You telling me what to do?"

"I'm trying to keep us out of trouble. That's why I'll lead the way in. They may recognize me from passing through with Madden. Give me a better reception, me not being in uniform."

"Just one outlaw to another," Falk said.

Craig ignored the sarcasm and rode ahead into the short roadway that fronted the shacks.

Only one man was in sight, standing on a crude porch. He wore buckaroo clothes, and a gun hung on his hip.

Falk said, "Where are the rest of them?"

"Watching from inside the shacks," Craig said. "Don't make any crazy moves, Captain."

He rode up to the waiting man, with his right palm raised.

The buckaroo gave him a long stare, and a hint of recognition showed on his face.

Then he turned his attention to Falk. "Ain't no Injun trouble in these parts, Cap'n."

"We're just passing through," Craig said.

"To where?"

Falk said, "That's not information of concern to you."

"It might be," the rustler said. "Ain't often we see cavalry here."

Craig said, "All we ask is to water our horses and fill our canteens. And to make camp down the road a piece."

The rustler thought about this before he spoke. Then he said, "All right." He studied Craig curiously. "You riding scout for this patrol?"

"Yeah," Craig said.

"I find that strange," the rustler said.

"I find it that way myself," Craig said. He touched heels to his mount, turning away, the others following suit.

"You pull out, come morning," the rustler called. "We got damn little grazing left to spare."

"We'll ride, first thing," Craig said.

"Be best," the rustler said.

They got water from the stream, then moved on down the trail a mile to bivouack.

"Suspicious character," Falk said.

"Wouldn't you be, in his business?"

"If I had time, I'd give him good reason," Falk said.

"He suspects that, no doubt," Craig said. "One reason he wants us out of here quick."

"He knew you," Falk said, sounding as if it were an accusation.

"Of course he did. He's seen me riding with Madden," Craig said, irritated by Falk's tone, "I recall seeing him, too."

"Birds of a feather," Falk said.

Craig fought down his temper. It was bad enough the way he felt about what he was doing. And Falk had a way of making it worse.

In the morning, the land south of the rustler settlement gradually became desert. Beyond, though, they could see the rise of a mountain.

"That's where we're headed," Craig said. "That's the north end of the Needle range. Place called Chisco Springs."

"Madden's lair?" Falk said.

"Him and several other hard characters who were there before him."

Falk said, "With a couple of squads, I could clean out the rustlers back there as well as the lawbreakers ahead."

"Making plans, Captain? You better see how you make out with Madden first."

Falk made no comment on this. But presently he said, "When we catch up—with Madden, I mean—where will you stand?"

"Neutral," Craig said.

"Neutral? Even after they shot you?"

"One man shot me," Craig said. "Slack. But the real reason I'm with this detail is to stop the killing of the stage guards and drivers."

"You trying to sound noble?"

"Nothing noble about it," Craig said.

Falk stared at him shrewdly. "Can I depend on you then to use your weapon against them?"

"No," Craig said.

"No? You wouldn't fire on them?"

"I didn't say that. I said you couldn't depend on me to do it."

"What does that mean?"

"It means I'm not certain, Captain."

Falk was silent, then nodded. "I expected that. It's another example of your letting your emotions interfere with your duty. Same thing that got you into trouble in the first place."

They approached the beginning of the mountain range.

"Getting close," Craig said.

Falk said, "Those other outlaws living there, will they join with Madden against us?"

"That's a good question," Craig said. "But I don't think so. Madden was keeping apart from them, and they seemed to like it that way. It's pretty much a case of live-and-let-live there. A just-don't-interfere-in-anybody-else's-business, and take-care-of-your-own sort of place." He paused, considering further the question, then added, "I'd guess the other hard-cases, like the rustlers of Garrison, don't like the idea of tangling with army troops. Not only because fighting is the army's business, but because any set-to with an army unit could bring on a bigger force. They're not likely to risk that."

"Good," Falk said.

"But you still got to match Madden, man for man. You will remember, Captain, they once fought under your command."

"They were soldiers then," Falk said. "Under discipline.

That's what makes a soldier." He paused. "Now they are deserters, freebooters without the pride that discipline instills—desperados thinking only of their own skins. They have thrown away their greatest asset."

"They are still under Madden's hand," Craig said.

"The worst of the bunch," Falk said. "By now, he has learned that it is the insignia and authority of rank that makes a soldier reach beyond himself in action."

For a moment Craig wondered if, for once, Falk had said something true. Madden was still a leader, but he no longer had the clout he'd had as first sergeant. Now his men were apt to argue a bit if they differed with him. Thinking back, he realized that this had been a growing thing, even at the time that Craig had left them.

"These men with me now," Falk said, "are soldiers, not deserters, and that is what will make the difference in a showdown."

"I wouldn't be too sure," Craig said.

"Because you are not a soldier anymore," Falk said.

"That was not my decision," Craig said, and waited for Falk's rebuttal.

He was surprised when it did not come.

Falk was silent, not looking at him. His face could not be read, but there was a slight frown there.

As if he were a man who wondered if an act in his past might have been a mistake. As if he were a man capable of regret.

The day after his argument with Slack at Chisco Springs, Madden described a new project. Increasing restlessness of his men had brought him to it sooner than he had planned.

"I've got something different in mind," he said.

He was speaking to Hiller.

Hiller said, "Different?"

"Different from stagecoaches."

They were sitting together at a table in the Chisco saloon.

The place was empty except for them and the bar owner who was checking his stock behind the bar.

"Hell, we're doing all right with coaches," Hiller said.

"Keep your voice down," Madden said. He nodded in the direction of the barman. "We can't trust anybody in this town."

"What you got in mind?"

"A bank."

"A bank!" Hiller's voice came louder than he intended.

"Dammit, man, keep it down!"

Hiller lowered his voice. "Where?"

"Pioche."

"Why Pioche?"

"Where else is there a bank that close?"

"I didn't know they had one there," Hiller said.

"I learned about it from one of these owlhooters. Once a bank robber himself. Got to talking too much the other night while I was buying him drinks. I think he's got half a mind to try a hit on it himself. Trouble is, he's a loner, and getting old. His nerve is gone."

"How much money they keep in a bank in a place like Pioche?" Hiller said.

Madden shrugged. "I don't know that. But what gave me the idea was something else he said. While he was there recently, he heard the mine companies are trying to cut their payroll risks by making fewer shipments."

"They do that," Hiller said, "they got to make bigger amounts in shipments."

"Exactly. Instead of weekly stage runs, men like Crowell are shipping monthly and depositing the larger amount in the bank, to be drawn each week as needed."

"Why not just hit the single big shipment?" Hiller said.

"How would we know when it would be? Camp along the route for a month trying to pick it?"

Hiller had no answer.

"This way, we know that most of the month the bank has

anywhere from one month's wages on deposit down to at least a final weekly draw. And with all the mine companies doing likewise, we stand a chance of making a killing that could let us all retire."

"Retire?" Hiller said. "I like that idea, Sarge. And I think most of the men would feel likewise."

PART IV

A Common Enemy

CHAPTER 13

LONE Horse, a war chief of the Gosiutes, was dissatisfied.

This, even though he had again escaped a force sent from Fort Halleck to pursue him and his band of marauders; a force he believed was still north of the Humboldt River, futilely searching for him.

Such escapes had become routine and no longer brought him the titillation they once had. This was not due to lack of effort on the part of the soldiers who hounded him after nearly every attack he made on a ranch or small mine camp or freight shipment. It was due, he knew, to his own cunning in eluding them.

He was just shrewder than they were, he thought.

He had reached a point, in his physical prime at the age of thirty-two, where he desired to gamble on a higher-stakes game. One that, if he won, would put his name on every Indian tongue in Nevada, not only Gosiute, but Shoshone and Paiute as well.

He longed now to become famed as the greatest warrior of the Great Basin country. To be the area champion of the red race against the whites.

What greater honor could a man desire?

For many months now he had sought a way to accomplish this goal. And he came to feel that to do it he must enter a new field. A plan began to form in his mind when he heard what was happening southward, in the area of the white man's rich strikes of silver.

The word was brought to him by an emissary sent by a Gosiute band of that area. He came asking for Lone Horse to help them with their problem. It was a request that, in turn, showed him how to achieve his own end. It had to do with the gathering of pinenuts.

The emissary, a young brave called Buck who had in his boyhood years lived with and worked for a white rancher in a sort of patron-slave relationship and knew of their ways, laid it out for him.

"Our people face starvation for the coming winter because our forests of nut pines have been nearly destroyed by the whites. Destroyed to feed the ovens they use to make charcoal to fuel the furnaces in what they call their smelters."

"It must take many nut pines, if the forests are being destroyed," Lone Horse said.

"Many," Buck said. "In white man's numbers, it goes like this—a full cord of pine wood makes only enough charcoal to smelt a single ton of silver ore."

"And how big is a cord?" Lone Horse said.

"A small nut pine will not make a cord," Buck said. "But you can think maybe one tree, one cord, one ton of ore."

"And how many tons of ore?"

"At the place called Pioche, I have heard they mine over a hundred tons a day, maybe more."

"How many men in this place you speak of?"

"What I heard, maybe two thousand, maybe more, maybe not so many."

"I am glad to know the exact number," Lone Horse said. He was not without humor.

"Will you help us?" Buck said.

Lone Horse was already thinking about it. He would need a big force to do what he was considering.

Why not draw from the other tribes of the basin, he thought. The Paiutes and the Shoshones were always rivals, sometimes even enemies, but if he could include them in the force he led, it would even more quickly spread his reputation.

With their aid, he would raid the town of Pioche, and attain his grand ambition for fame.

He would need to impress on them that this was their chance to deal out retribution to the whites. It might even cause the whites to stop devastating the Indian source of sustenance.

He did not really believe that would happen. But he felt he had enough ability as an orator to convince them it could. He would play on their emotions, not their logic.

Whether his raid accomplished this or not did not greatly concern him. Becoming famous did. This could be the chance he had been looking for.

And something of this kind of action had lain latent in his mind for many months.

He had already been thinking of contacting Red Knife, a chief of a Shoshone band across the ranges to the west.

Hunger among the Indians of Nevada was endemic, a major motivation for their depredations. And now, with the word brought by Buck of the increased onslaughts on the nut pine forests, Lone Horse was certain the other tribes in the mining districts were suffering likewise.

This was the season for harvesting the nuts, and if the harvest was meager, malnutrition was faced by all. For many, even starvation in the coming winter.

"I will help," Lone Horse said. "And you will help me to act at once, lending truth to my mission, as you are one who is familiar with this present ruthless behavior of the whites."

"It will give me pleasure to act as your aide," Buck said.

"Then we will now cross the range to the west and speak to the Shoshone leader, Red Knife."

"Will he join us?"

"We will see. I will attack the whites, regardless."

"If you do this thing," Buck said, "your praises will be sung by many."

Lone Horse shook his head. "I do not do it for praise," he said solemnly. "I will do it for the welfare of our people."

They crossed the mountains to the west and came to the valley where the Shoshones of Red Knife's band existed.

They had once met, and in spite of a tribal wariness the Shoshone received Lone Horse courteously, recalling stories he had heard recently of the Gosiute's harassing of whites and his outwitting of the troops of Fort Halleck. Stories that came through the greasewood and sagebrush telegraph of the Great Basin.

Seated in his wickiup of brush and rabbit skins, he listened as Lone Horse outlined his plan.

"We will bring vengeance down on these destroyers of our orchards," Lone Horse said. Orchards were what the Indians considered their nut pine forests to be.

"We will strike a blow," he continued, "that will inspire our people everywhere and that will put a fear into the whites of ravaging our food supply."

"And what is it you ask of me?" Red Knife said.

"I ask that you send warriors to fight beside my own, so that the whites will know this is a united revolt against their tyranny, a unity of all Indians of the basin country."

"How many warriors?"

"Twenty-five would be a good number. I will match them with an equal number of mine."

"Fifty warriors would be enough?"

"I will go to the Paiutes and ask them to join us, too."

"Yes," Red Knife said. "The Paiutes are many in number. We Shoshones do not always get along with them for that reason. But perhaps in this we can."

"Against a common enemy, you must," Lone Horse said.

"Where will our forces meet?"

"The dry lake called by the whites Gosiute," Lone Horse said. "That would be a good place."

"It will be done."

"We will meet there in a week. Send your young warriors with their best arms. Will you come with them?"

Red Knife was silent. Then he said, "I have many years on me. My spirit is willing. My body, though, does not respond as it did in my youth."

Lone Horse nodded. "I understand. And it is best that our warriors be young. The young fight best, but I will lead them."

"I will tell them to obey your commands in battle," Red Knife said.

"At the meeting place then, within the week."

"It will be done. My young men will be glad to fight. They long always for action."

"They will get it," Lone Horse said.

Lone Horse and Buck now turned south and traveled to the country of Tempiute Jim of the Paiutes.

Chief Jim's band roamed a region southwest of Pioche, in an area north of Tempiute Range.

The Paiute chief was of Lone Horse's age and somewhat of his temperament. There was similarity, too, in their hatred of the whites and their longing for fame. They differed in that Lone Horse had progressed considerably further in his ambition.

Jim had heard of Lone Horse's successful exploits, but the reverse was barely true. Their meeting was more constrained than had been that of Lone Horse with the Shoshone chieftain.

However, Buck had counseled Lone Horse on what to expect, having learned by hearsay of Chief Jim's big ego.

And Lone Horse, wanting reinforcements from the Paiute band, hid his disaffection at the Paiute's manner, which contained none of the respect he felt was his due.

Even from the first, though, there was no problem with getting a promise of help from Jim. The problem arose when Jim suggested that he be the one to lead the attacking force.

"I have been there, in the town, many times," he said. "My knowledge of the streets could be of great use."

"You can be at my side," Lone Horse said. "You can impart this knowledge to me then. But it is I who will lead."

Buck, who knew well the ambition of Tempiute Jim, spoke soothingly and with deference to the Paiute.

"There will be glory to share between the two of you, both being great men of your people. But, since Lone Horse is father of the idea, it is only right, is it not, that he should lead the party of war?"

Tempiute Bill looked unconvinced.

"There is always the chance that the leader will fall," Buck said. "And you would then take command."

The Paiute chief thought about this, then finally nodded.

"So be it," he said.

In an attack on the town of the whites, he was thinking, anything could happen. Lone Horse could very well be a casualty. There would be a lot of bullets and arrows flying around.

Tempiute Jim thought about that and looked forward to it. He had a brand-new rifle he had recently stolen from a hardware store in the town of Hiko.

"And where will we join our war parties?" he said.

"I will be coming from Gosiute Lake with my people and Red Knife's Shoshones," Lone Horse said. "But to make it easy for you, we will meet on the White River at the north end of Pah Rock Range, near the fork of Valley Creek. From there, with a short march, we can descend upon the town with great surprise to the whites."

"It shall be done," Tempiute Jim said.

I am the right man at the rigtht time, Lone Horse was thinking. *The times call for a man of my ability.*

The opportunity was there as it had not been since 1860, when the Paiutes from all over Nevada gathered at big Pyramid Lake in western Nevada to hold a council. The purpose was to protest the encroachment of the whites, who were taking the Paiute horse-grazing lands to run their cattle, killing the game, and cutting the forests to shore their mines. That gathering of the tribe led indirectly to an assault upon them by a force of volunteer whites under the command of a Major Ormsby. Outnumbered, the whites met with disaster, and Ormsby was killed. It was a great victory for the Paiutes, and for a while afterward encouraged smaller uprisings among the tribes.

Lone Horse, at that time in his young manhood, far to the east in the Gosiute country, had heard what happened at Pyramid Lake and was thrilled by it.

But his interest, even then, went far beyond the excitement of the news. His interest settled on the subsequent rise to renown of various scattered chiefs who dared to continue in lesser conflicts with the whites.

Some of their names he could still readily recall.

There had been Black Rock Tom, a Paiute, whose own band was joined by Shoshones and Bannocks, who kept the area to the northwest in turmoil for a time.

And later there had been Big Foot, a Shoshone, rampaging in Paradise Valley. And there had been others.

And, more important, there had been White Horse of the Gosiutes, Lone Horse's mentor by observance and near identical namesake, under whose leadership he had served an apprenticeship in depredation.

It had been in 1863 that they began their hostilities by killing the Overland Stage relay-station keeper at Eight-Mile Station near the Utah border. This was on the transcontinental stage route that followed the old Pony Express route.

On that day in March the Overland stagecoach came barreling into the station, a driver known as Happy Harry at the reins. There were four passengers in the coach, Judge G. N. Mott of Nevada, and an old man on his way home to the East from California, with his two little sons at his sides.

The Indians greeted its arrival with a hail of bullets and arrows.

Happy Harry took a mortal wound, but kept his frightened team racing down the road.

Inside the coach, the old man, pierced by an arrow, sank onto the floor.

Up on the box, the driver fought to retain consciousness as he urged the horses on. Nearing his end, he called down for help.

Judge Mott responded, climbing up the side of the speeding, lurching coach to reach the dying driver's side and grab the reins as the latter fell dead into the front boot.

Judge Mott reached the next station at Deep Creek with the corpse, the wounded old man who later recovered, and the two little boys.

The Gosiutes had not followed. Instead, they burned Eight-Mile Station, drove off the stock, and began a period of raids that became known as the Overland War.

Within a few days there were other incidents of war along the whole Overland Stage route from Salt Lake City to Schell Creek, Nevada, a distance of 225 miles. Three days after the death of Happy Harry, Company K, Second California Infantry Volunteers, Captain S. P. Smith in command, was marching from Fort Douglas, Utah, for the scene of the disaster. They were posted later at an outpost known as Camp Ruby, miles to the west across Schell Creek.

By early May, Company E, Third California Infantry Volunteers, left Fort Douglas to guard the Overland route between Salt Lake and the mining town of Austin in Central Nevada, four soldiers being left at each station.

As a stage arrived at a station, two of the soldiers posted there would ride as guards to the next station, then guard the next return stage back.

This left the cavalry patrols out of Camp Ruby free to scout through the country and patrol the road.

Soon after the destruction of Eight-Mile Station, a stage was ambushed at night as it drove through a canyon just east of Schell Creek. There were seven passengers aboard, two of them women. Fortunately the other five were soldiers.

The Indian attack was repelled, and the coach got through

before having to stop when one of the horses dropped dead from multiple wounds—one of the few incidents during this time that did not bring disaster to the whites.

A few weeks later, a stage passing through another canyon, east of Deep Creek Station, was fired upon from the rocky heights. The driver, Riley Simpson, was shot off his seat, mortally wounded.

The guard on the box beside him seized the lines and kept the coach racing on. A chase of many miles ensued, but he eventually eluded the band of attacking Gosiutes.

Eight miles east of this, near the Utah line, was Canyon Station, which had to be supplied with water hauled by wagon from nearby Deep Creek Slough.

The Indians had burned this station, killed the man in charge, and driven off the stock on the day following the death of Happy Harry.

At this point four soldiers were sent down from Fort Douglas, Utah, to act as guards. Besides these four, two men were there to take care of the Overland Stage stock, one of them named Deaf Bill, the other his assistant.

During the last days of June, Privates Abbott and Hervey rode as stage guards on the run back from Deep Creek to their home station. They had been expecting trouble, and were relieved when none occurred.

As the stage continued unescorted into Utah, the two set out with Deaf Bill driving the wagon to get water from the slough. Privates Elliott and Burger remained with the assistant hostler to take care of the station. They had procured the water and were close to the station on their return, when a shot was fired and Hervey fell dead from his seat.

A second volley blasted from a screen of high sagebrush, hitting Abbott in the shoulder and knocking him from the wagon. One bullet cut off Deaf Bill's thumb. One struck a horse in the chest.

The horses bolted, but Deaf Bill stopped them and despite

his missing thumb, opened fire on the Gosiutes with a hand-gun he carried, dropping one.

Abbott sprang to his feet, spotted the Indians still lurking in brush, and made a run for the wagon. He grabbed up his rifle and commenced firing.

The Indians fired back, wounding him in both legs, but despite this he rushed toward the body of his comrade, not realizing he was dead, pulled him up, and staggered back to throw him and himself into the wagon bed as Deaf Bill whipped the horse into a run for the station. But two more bullets struck Abbott, one in each side.

They were met there by the assistant hostler, alone, who had heard the shooting. Elliott and Burger, he told them, had gone out hunting sage hens after the water party left.

Looking toward a knoll in the direction taken by the missing men, Abbott saw the glistening barrel of Elliott's rifle in the possession of a Gosiute and knew then that the men were dead.

The Indians opened fire again, but as sometimes occurred when satisfied with the casualties inflicted, they soon stopped and inexplicably rode off.

A half hour later, an emigrant train came into the station, bringing the body of Elliott, which had been found a short distance from there. With the emigrants, fortunately, there was a surgeon, who dressed Abbott's five wounds, saving his life.

The next day Burger's body was found on a hillside, probably a first victim. His body showed evidence of a des-perate running fight. And he had been badly mutilated, his whiskers torn from his face in place of scalping, since he was bald. His heart had been cut out.

In July, another attack was made on the same station.

There were now another four soldiers there, once again sent down from Fort Douglas, Utah, as replacements for the casualties.

They were Privates Grimshaw, McNamara, Myers, and Pratt.

Deaf Bill, his thumb wound slowly healing, was still on duty as hostler, as was his assistant. He was in front of the barn, currying a horse, when a shot was fired from the surrounding cover, killing him instantly.

At the sound, the assistant hostler ran out of the barn, and one of the soldiers rushed from a dugout they had been using as a camp. Both were shot down.

The other three privates made a run for the barn, and one was killed as they ran.

There were now only two left to continue the fight. Once in the barn, they dragged up sacks of grain to make a breastwork; for an hour they were able to keep their concealed foes at bay.

By now they knew the enemies were Gosiutes, verified by a flaming arrow that landed in a pile of hay near the barn and set the dry timbers afire. The flames spread furiously. Desperately the two men fought to saddle a couple of panicked horses that chanced to be in the barn.

Then, under a hail of bullets and arrows, they spurred out of the burning structure. They reached the road, still running a gauntlet of weapon fire from the cover of the bordering sagebrush.

They raced down the road, pulling almost out of range of the bullets. Myers suddenly threw up his hands and fell from the saddle, bouncing as he struck the hard-packed roadway. His horse staggered onward for a few paces, then it too went down. Both were dead.

Pratt made it a few yards farther before he and his horse were felled. Both lay still.

Later that day another emigrant train, passing through on its way to California, came upon them. The horse was dead. Pratt was dying.

He lived only long enough to tell them, weakly, what had happened.

And so, for a time, the raids of the Gosiutes had gone on. Then, gradually, the army had regained control.

But during that brief period the loss to the Overland Stage Company from this warfare of the Gosiutes was nearly two hundred horses, seven stations burned, sixteen men killed, and countless others wounded.

It was a time to look back upon with relish, Lone Horse was thinking. It was a time that inspired him for what he was now about to do.

CHAPTER 14

A MILE from the outlaw town, Craig said, "Best to stop here, Captain. "The place is just beyond that cluster of pines."

"What's the size of it?"

"Three or four times as big as Garrison," Craig said.

"That include Madden's deserters?"

"No. Besides them."

"You say they won't side with Madden?"

"I said I didn't think so."

"All right. Lead the way in."

"Not hardly, Captain. I've brought you to them. This is as far as I go."

"I might have known," Falk said.

"I've had time to think on this," Craig said. "If I lead you in, any one of the bunch will likely shoot me out of the saddle." He paused. "Can't say I'd blame them, either."

"Lost your guts, eh?"

"May be, Captain. But not my mind. They may hesitate to open fire on a squad of uniformed cavalry, for one reason or another. But that won't hold true for me."

Falk looked thoughtful. Then, surprisingly, he said, "I guess I understand."

He turned to the troopers, still holding in the short column of twos, and gave his command, "Squad right into line."

The men moved into a skirmish line, and each unstudded the flap of his revolver holster. Each knew what was coming.

"Return fire, if fired upon," Falk said. "Squad, forward—march!"

They rode toward the trees that hid the town.

Craig watched and shook his head, but he knew that disciplined formality of approach was what he should expect from Falk.

He wondered if Madden's defense would be as formal. Would the old army drill take over in his commands as well, or had the recent months of outlaw living lessened it?

He sat his mount, listening now for the sound of guns that might give him the answer.

Captain Falk rode erect in his saddle as they passed around the cover of pines and entered the town. He felt exposed, but he would not cringe. Exposure to potential bullets went with an officer's profession.

The street was empty. On either side Falk scrutinized the line of structures. As Craig had told him, the town was like the one at Garrison, except that there was some timber around it and some of the buildings were built of logs. And the town was bigger.

Falk felt a growing dread at its desertion.

He had hoped to march in and confront his quarry. Now he was fearfully aware that he was open to ambush.

Fearfully and foolishly, though he fought against admitting this to himself.

He was momentarily at a loss for a next move, and he had an uneasy feeling the squad from Fort Halleck sensed this.

The disturbing situation suddenly cleared for him, as a hardcase gunman stepped out on a porch. Falk had a quick sense of déjà vu. This too had happened at Garrison.

The gunman sized up the squad with a sweeping glance, then faced Falk.

"You looking for somebody?"

"Not your kind," Falk said.

"My kind is the only ones here," the gunman said.

Falk thought about that.

The gunman then said, "Your kind are strangers."

Falk said, "I'm looking for a bunch that may still have an army look about them."

"Damned if they don't," the gunman said.

"They're here then?"

"Been and gone, Captain. And good riddance, I'd say."

"Gone where?"

"Couldn't say."

"Gone when?"

"Couldn't say that neither."

Falk showed his irritation. "Couldn't or wouldn't?" he said.

"Amounts to the same thing, Captain."

"You sounded like you were glad they've gone."

"A true fact, Captain," the gunman said. "But that fact don't make no difference."

From the doorway behind him stepped a small, wiry old man who staggered as he stepped, then stood weaving unsteadily, his legs spread. "Damn well makes a difference to me, Lieutenant," he said.

He looked drunk, Falk thought.

"This here is a captain," the gunman said.

"Still makes a difference," the drunk said.

"What do you mean by that?" Falk said, alert.

"I mean that son of a bitch they all call Sarge, he done rode off without him taken me along."

"Why would he do that?" Falk said.

"Why? He done it so's to beat me out of a share of the loot."

"Shut up!" the gunman said.

"Shut up, hell!" the drunk said. "They left me here and all rode off to rob the Miners Bank in Pioche. And that after me telling them how to do it."

The gunman stepped toward him, his hand doubled into a fist.

Falk jerked out his army Colt. "Hold it!"

He was too late, as the gunman threw a hard punch aimed

behind the drunk's ear. But at that moment the drunk's knees buckled slightly, and the punch missed.

"Hold it!" Falk commanded again.

This time the gunman looked around and saw Falk's weapon covering him.

"You little snitch!" he said to the drunk, but he held as Falk had ordered.

The drunk said to Falk, "If you're after that frigging sergeant and them deserters, you take the trail to Pioche and ride fast, and by God you'll catch them."

The gunman said to the drunk, "You're through in this town."

The drunk seemed not to hear, or was drunk enough not to care.

Falk thought, *He'll be caring later. As soon as we ride out.*

He said then to the squad, "You heard the man," and turned away from the porch and toward the pines where Craig was waiting. He glanced over his shoulder as the troopers fell in behind.

He saw the two men still on the porch. The gunman had his weapon out now. He was pistol-whipping the drunk.

Craig had been watching from the cover of the trees.

He said, "Well?"

Before Falk could answer, Barlow said, "Captain, they could have been lying."

Falk said, "The gunman, maybe. But the drunk I have to believe. It rang too true to be an act."

"What's he talking about?" Craig said.

Falk explained.

"So you think Madden has gone?"

"I believe it enough to take a chance. If they are gone, the drunk said we could overtake them by riding fast." He paused. "If that's so, we can't afford to waste time here."

Craig said, "And if they did fool you with an act, Captain—?"

Falk gave him a cold look. "I do not fool easily," he said. "We will take to the trail at once. Do you know it?"

"I have been over it once," Craig said.

"Lead the way, then."

Craig found the trace west of the town, and Falk set an alternate walk and trot pace with brief hourly breaks to breathe the mounts.

Craig was concerned. It was a long way to Pioche.

He said, "You keep this up, and if we don't catch Madden soon you'll tire the horses."

"Are you trying to tell me what a cavalry mount will do?"

"Not telling. Just reminding," Craig said. "I know how bad you want to catch him. That might make you forget."

"Madden should have no reason to hurry," Falk said. "Let's see what the signs show us as we go along."

That sounded reasonable enough to Craig, and he said, unthinking, "Very well, sir." His reply brought a searching look from Falk.

Signs soon appeared in the form of horse droppings ahead of them. They were only partially dry.

"Not over a couple of hours old, I'd say," Falk said.

Craig agreed.

Then, as they maintained their gait, the droppings became increasingly less dry.

Falk himself finally dismounted to make an inspection after Craig had several times done so.

"Not much more than an hour ahead," Falk said.

"I agree."

"How far would you say we are from Pioche?"

"Half the distance from Chisco. Twenty, twenty-five miles yet to go," Craig said. "At the risk of making you mad, Captain, I'll say our mounts have about had it. You got to remember they covered probably fifteen miles from Garrison this morning before we got to Chisco.

"I'm aware of that," Falk said. "I'm also aware that Madden's horses have fifteen miles less on them. But if we stop now, he'll regain his original lead."

"Look around you, Captain," Craig said. "It's approaching dusk. And as you yourself said, he's got no use to hurry. So he'll be making camp for the night. I suggest we do that, too, and try to catch him in the morning."

"For an ex-private, you're damned free with your suggestions," Falk said.

"Comes from being a civilian, Captain. It's your decision to make."

"I was about to," Falks said testily. "We'll bivouack here."

With forty miles in the saddle that day, the tired troopers dismounted gratefully and set about making camp.

Falk had them up at first light, and a half hour later they were on their way, again setting a fast pace.

Within an hour they came to the deserted campsite of their quarry.

Falk said, "If we'd kept on we'd have surprised them in camp last night. Now it looks like they may have pulled out before dawn. If so, we've lost some of our gain."

"We've not lost much, and now we have rested horses," Craig said.

Falk did not acknowledge the statement. Instead, he said, "All right, let's get on with it, then."

Presently, as they rode, he said, "You've worked in Pioche. Do you know where the Miners Bank is?"

"Yes. Near the joining of Main and Lacour Streets."

"That's the one they intend to rob."

"I guessed that," Craig said. "It's the only one."

His comment brought back Falk's frown, but he only said, "We've got to catch them before they get there."

Madden's nerves were on edge. He had never robbed a bank before, and he was certain none of his men had either.

He wondered whether it was a mistake not to include the old derelict bank robber in on this.

He had left the drunk behind because the oldster had impressed him as worthless except for talk. Besides, you never knew what a rummy like that might do. You couldn't depend on him.

But now he was having second thoughts. The oldster's experience and expertise, if valid, might have been worth a share of the take, he thought. But how did you know how much of a drunkard's rambling was true, and how much was just alcoholic bluster?

Which was something else to worry about.

Maybe the whole idea was based on the imaginings of a soused brain. The thought did not improve Madden's feelings any.

He was suddenly impatient to get it over with. He had been keeping to an easy pace; knowing the trail and having got an early start, he figured to reach their destination about noon. But now his impatience drove him to order an occasional trot. Even though it might be unwise—considering they'd need to make a fast getaway after the holdup—it brought a relief to him he found difficult to forego.

The men were impatient, too. They were eager for the big haul that would, as Hiller had put it to them, allow them to retire. They were already making plans as they rode.

"Me," Snyder said, "I'm going to take my share and maybe open a saloon."

Hiller, now riding beside him, said, "Hell, Snyder, you'd drink up the profits yourself."

Some of the others laughed, which made Snyder surly, and he said, "Some of us can handle likker, and some of us can't."

"Sure, Snyder, that's just what I was saying."

There was another round of laughter.

Snyder bridled. "What the hell you mean by that?"

Hiller knew when to back off. He didn't reply.

Slack, always truculent, said, "Yeah, Snyder, you and Parrett ought to go partners."

"Mind your mouth!" Parrett said. "Nobody accuses me of being a lush."

Slack, enjoying his reaction, made things worse by not answering.

"You hear what I said?" Parrett said.

Hiller, realizing he had started something that could lead to trouble, sought to ease the tension. He said, "What I want is a comfortable place to live. A big soft armchair instead of this ball-breaking saddle."

Bentley said, "That sounds good to me too, Hiller. I'd like to live a life of calm contemplation and poetic ease."

"Listen to that!" Hiller said. "What the hell does it mean?"

"I don't rightly know," Bentley said. "I must have read it somewheres."

"What about you, Slack?" Hiller said.

"What about what?"

"What do you intend to do with your share of the bank's holdings?"

"Get away from you bastards, as far as I can," Slack said.

His remark made them all fall silent.

The strain held until Hoch said, "Me. I figure maybe to open a whorehouse."

His words brought a few chuckles, but the quiet among them continued as they rode.

Madden, thinking about what they'd said, pondered what his own future might be.

The trail here led through rough, mountainous country, which made for hard riding, but that could be an advantage, he thought, if they should later be pursued by a citizen posse. It was also good terrain in which to form an ambush, if necessary, although he hoped such would not be the case.

He was against killing. He was not a bloodthirsty man. He'd tried to impress on his men that killing aroused adverse public sentiment.

Like Craig, he had killed as a soldier, but not wantonly.

And the blood that had been shed during their recent exploits laid heavily on him.

Its weight, in fact, had helped bring him to the decision to rob the bank, in the hope the proceeds would be big enough to let him comfortably withdraw from the criminal career on which he now wished he'd never embarked.

He was beginning to feel it had been a mistake to desert his army career. His present life had not provided the satisfaction he had expected.

He missed now the feel of importance he'd had as first sergeant of Company D. And even though he still gave the orders, he was aware of increasing dissatisfaction among his men. He wondered now if some of them also were having second thoughts.

Maybe Craig had been the smart one, after all, getting out while he could.

That thought brought him up abruptly, as it had repeatedly since he'd last seen Craig lying unconscious across the floor of the stagecoach, gushing blood. He wondered again if Craig had survived. He wondered if he'd ever know.

He gave his head a savage shake. He had to get a grip on himself.

Hiller, riding beside him again, noticed his strange action and said, "What's wrong, Sarge? You got a headache?"

"Yeah, I got one," Madden said shortly.

Hiller considered this and rode briefly in silence.

Madden again gave them the command to proceed at a trot.

Captain Falk's horse came up lame as they began a descent from the high trail through the Wilson Range.

They were moving fast when it happened.

It was Falk's own fault, Craig thought.

They had come to a stretch of trail filled with loose rock, and instead of breaking the gait, Falk, eager to close in on the deserters, held to a trot. Craig had just opened his mouth to warn of the danger when it happened.

Falk's mount stepped on a small rounded boulder, stumbled, and almost went down.

Falk, startled, jerked up on the reins. The mount regained its footing, but went into a severe limp.

The column came to a halt, the troopers staring at Falk.

His face was set at this new frustration. He dismounted, bent down, and felt at the left fetlock. The joint was already swelling.

"Tough luck, Captain," Craig said.

Falk looked up at him. He appeared as if he'd like to blame Craig for this but knew he couldn't.

"Ain't likely we'll overtake them now," Barlow said to Private Wilkes.

Falk overheard him.

"Barlow, dismount," he said. "I'll ride your horse."

"Mine, sir?"

"Yours."

"You going to leave me here, sir?"

"You may be able to ride mine at a walk."

"I ain't familiar with this trail or terrain, sir."

"That's hardly new for you, is it?" Falk said.

"If the horse gets worse lame, sir, I'll be stranded in these mountains. And you won't be coming back this way, will you?"

Falk hesitated, and Craig said, "He could ride double with somebody."

"It would slow us down," Falk said. But he appeared to give it thought. He knew Major Forrest would take a dim view of the abandonment of one of his troopers.

"Your decision, Captain," Craig said.

Falk considered a moment longer, then said, "Barlow, you mount up behind Wilkes. You can lead the lame mount. We'll see—it may recover."

"Yes, sir," Barlow said with some relief.

Wilkes did not appear to share his feeling. "Begging your pardon, sir, but riding double we can't keep a fast gait."

"I'm aware of that," Falk said. "We'll go on ahead. You follow as best you can."

Craig said in a low voice, "That leaves you two men short when you close in on Madden."

"I told you it's discipline that will make the difference," Falk said. "Soldiers against deserters. You'll see an example of that."

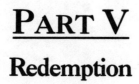

PART V

Redemption

CHAPTER 15

TRUE to his promise, the Shoshone chief, Red Knife, sent his warriors to the area of the dry lake, where Lone Horse's Gosiutes waited.

Together they moved southward to the rendevous and met with Tempiute Jim and his Paiutes on the White River near Valley Creek.

They were now some seventy-five strong, all of them eager for action.

Tempiute Jim immediately attached himself to Lone Horse, making it known to all that he was second in command.

He had with him the new rifle he had stolen from the hardware store in Hiko and was yearning to use it.

I will be a big man when this is over, he thought. And it is only right that it be so, because I am a Paiute. And always we have been greater than the others.

Even before the whites came to settle, we had subjugated the Shoshones and exacted tribute from them, and we only allowed them to keep a small number of ponies to each band. That was how we kept their young men dismounted so we could control them.

And we took away by force the attractive Shoshone maidens for our own lodges.

Then the white men came to settle and became our biggest problem, and we no longer had the will to control the Shoshones. And they came to believe they were as good as we Paiutes. They came to believe this when they saw how the white men dominated us.

But now this will change. I, Tempiute Jim, say it.

The braves of each tribe kept to themselves as they waited at the north end of Pah Rock Range. They would fight together, but they did not entirely trust each other. They would fight together against the whites because they distrusted the whites far more.

They would fight together to save, among other things, the nut pine forests.

Tempiute Jim said now to Lone Horse, "My warriors are impatient. We have been here several days, waiting. Waiting and wondering if you had lost your courage. Now that you are here, let us commence. Let us descend upon the town of Pioche and attack."

Lone Horse, stung by such rudeness from a Paiute, said, "You know better. If you are not deaf, you have heard of my raids on the ranches of the whites and on their freight wagons. You know well of the earlier Gosiute assaults on the Overland Stage Company by White Horse, under whose orders I, as a young man, took part."

"I have heard," Tempiute Jim said. "And I am tired of hearing. So let us make this raid of our own. Let us make this new act of war, to be discussed and praised from wickiup to wickiup throughout the Great Basin country."

"Get your men mounted," Lone Horse said, angered by the Paiute's words. "We will march on the town now."

They formed in tribal bunches and began their ride down a valley behind the low mountains that screened their approach from the people of Pioche.

Falk's decision to maintain his pace, leaving behind Barlow and Wilkes, was not a popular one with his men, as Craig soon sensed.

The troopers from Fort Halleck had served together long before Falk took them over, and their loyalties lay between them, not to this arrogant officer whom they scarcely knew.

Craig wondered if Falk had the sensitivity to realize this. Looking at him now, he saw no indication that it was so.

Now, as the double-riding pair dropped from sight, no longer visible to the backward glances of the remaining four troopers, Craig could hear open grumbling break out among them.

This caused him to again study Falk. The officer seemed still oblivious to the troopers' sentiments, staring ahead as if alert for some glimpse of their quarry.

Craig wondered at this. They were at a walk now, and Craig, riding beside Falk, could hear the words passed back and forth; it was hard to believe that Falk could not.

It was Private Starkey, the ex-Confederate Texan, who first voiced a complaint to his comrades. He had a southern accent that carried plainly, perhaps unknowingly. Or maybe not, Craig thought. From the beginning there had been a particular coolness between the officer and Starkey.

"Leaving two behind," Starkey said. "That leaves us with four to do the fighting against that deserter bunch of seven. Damn poor fighting odds, I'm thinking."

Dunnegan, who liked a fight, regardless of odds, said, "Five, including the captain."

"Even so," Starkey said.

Behind this pair, Private Gruber said with a German inflection, "The captain gives the orders. That is only right." But he did not sound as certain as he could have.

His companion, young Private Reed, who also liked action but had twice been wounded, said, "I would feel better if we had Wilkes and Barlow with us."

"As would any man with sense," Starkey said. "I seen enough poor-odds fighting in the war."

Falk turned suddenly in his saddle. He said to the Texan, "I understand you were in the Rebel army, trooper."

"*Rebel* army?" Starkey said. "I was in the Confederate States Army, suh."

"Under whom?"

"I fought under Sterling Price, suh. Texas Cavalry."

"Did they allow enlisted men to question the decisions of their officers in your army?" Falk said.

"Don't reckon they allowed it, suh. But it was done if the decisions was foolish."

"Ever stop to think that may have been why you lost the war?" Falk said.

"No, suh, I never did. Because I don't think that had anything to do with losing it. We lost because we had less of everything it takes to win. And that, suh, is what bothers me now. I mean, us being short of the two men we had."

Falk was again staring, eyes front, as if expecting to see Madden directly ahead. He seemed not to hear Starkey's words. Or if he did, he chose to ignore them.

It had surprised Craig that Falk had even condescended to the discussion with Private Starkey. That just wasn't like the man. It gave Craig worry. It was downright unnerving.

It made Craig wonder if Falk knew what the hell he was doing.

He reminded himself that he had no intention of getting actively into the fight with the deserters. Still, what would happen if Falk attacked shorthanded and the Fort Halleck troopers faced annihilation? Having heard Starkey's opinion, Craig thought this quite likely to happen.

Could he, Craig, stand by, refusing involvement, and see these U.S. Army men wiped out by the criminal bunch? If the deserter troop survived, they would know that he had led Falk to them and they would hunt him down.

He was now faced with the possibility he would have to join Falk in a fight to the death with his old comrades, in order to survive.

He felt sick at the thought. And then he asked himself what was different, really, than what he was now doing? What difference was there between personally going into combat against them or leading Falk's troopers to them for attack?

There is no difference, he thought. He felt unsettled and angry.

His anger again turned upon Falk, and he cursed him silently, and viciously. All that was happening to him now had begun with Falk.

And at that moment, he felt a bitterness so great that the possibility of Falk being among the dead casualties from the coming encounter was a most satisfying thought.

Madden's impatience grew, so that now he put his men steadily into the mile-eating trot and walk cavalry pace. It eased his nerves.

But it wasn't a wise move, considering the wear on the horses.

Hiller brought this to his attention. "We are not being followed," Hiller said.

"I know that," Madden said.

The way he said it caused Hiller to drop the subject. No use getting Madden riled, he was thinking. He'd been hard enough to get along with lately.

Ever since Craig got shot.

Hiller pondered this. Thinking back, it seemed that Sarge had always seemed to take a special interest in Craig. Almost like Craig was a son. Hiller supposed it was a natural feeling, Craig being the youngest man in the troop. The youngest, and the most eager learner.

It was too bad that goddam Falk hadn't taken a similar fatherly attitude. Army life had been hard enough without Falk's kind of officer.

Well, life under Falk was now behind them, he thought. There was a bright future ahead, just as soon as they cleaned out that bank in Pioche.

Thinking about it, Hiller grew impatient himself, glad that Madden had increased the pace. He wanted to get his hands on his share of that big money. He wanted to riffle it through his fingers.

He wanted to trade that McClellan saddle for an easy chair, and the sooner, the better.

Craig had been considering the trail sign with increased interest.

He said to Falk, "It looks like Madden is holding his own."

"What do you mean?" Falk said.

"Take another look at the tracks. He's riding a faster gait now."

Falk called a halt, dismounted, and pored over the hoof-prints in the trace. His mouth tightened.

For what reason?" he said. "He can't know we're behind him."

Craig shrugged.

"How far would you say we are from the town?" Falk said.

Craig thought about it, then said, "Ten, twelve miles maybe."

"I want to catch him before we reach it."

"You'll have to ride faster then."

"A smart observation," Falk said. "I'm glad to know." He climbed back into his saddle and sat there, thinking.

"Well, Captain?"

"Let's go," Falk said, and kicked his horse into a canter.

CHAPTER 16

OVER the months, the Nevada press had sporadically badgered Major Forrest for his apparent inability to stop the crime spree of the Deserter Troop.

When they elicited no verbal defense from the Fort Halleck commander, they renewed their barrage of criticism.

A reporter from the *Pioche Record,* returning by rail from Carson City, where he had been to take care of some business, decided to seek a personal interview with Major Forrest. He debarked at Halleck Station and was fortunate to catch the infrequent stage out to the fort. But he arrived there only to find that Major Forrest had taken to the field with a detachment to investigate a robbery of a Central Pacific express car, east of Wells.

"When do you expect him back?" he inquired of the major's orderly.

"I couldn't say, sir," the orderly said. "What was it you wanted to see him about?"

"I am with the *Pioche Record,* Corporal. A reporter. And, as the garrison here is the only one in our area, we take a civic interest in you as our protectors."

"I'm glad to hear that, sir," the corporal said.

"This robbery of the Central Pacific you mentioned—are there any suspects considered at this time?"

"Suspects?" the corporal said. "None that I know of, sir."

"It would seem likely to me that the notorious Deserter Troop might be considered," the reporter said.

"It's possible," the corporal said. "But no mention of such was made to me. Besides, Captain Falk is out searching again for that bunch somewhere south of here, along the Utah border."

The reporter's interest leaped, but he did not show it.

This was news, big news, but he only said, "And how is the captain doing with his search?"

"Hopefully he'll be doing better," the corporal said. "He has a new scout with him, who is supposed to know the country where they think the deserters' hideout is."

"I see," the reporter said. "This captain—Falk, is it?"

"Falk, yes, sir."

"This Falk, is he one of the major's picked officers?"

"Picked, sir?"

"I mean, is he experienced? Capable?"

"I suppose so, sir. Else why would he be given the assignment? But I couldn't say for sure. He's new here to the garrison. I understand, though, he is known to the major."

"Well," the reporter said, "I appreciate your information, corporal, although I'm sorry to have missed the major. I'll be catching the stage now, before it leaves to return to the station."

"Glad to be of help, sir," the corporal said. "And glad to hear you folks down in Pioche appreciate what we try to do here."

"Believe me, we do, Corporal," the reporter said.

It was only after the reporter left that the orderly realized he had given out information that Major Forrest might have been withholding from the press for a reason.

The reason being he did not want that bunch of deserters to know they were the object of a search-and-destroy mission.

The realization ruined the orderly's day.

The reporter, upon reaching Pioche, went immediately to the *Record* office and filed his story. He felt it was big news.

And so did his editor, who felt it so important that he

placed the edition carrying it at several special spots around town in addition to the regular circulation outlets.

Among them was a rack placed outside the front of the Miners Bank.

CHAPTER 17

THE Deserter Troop moved in at a trot as they reached the outskirts of Pioche.

Madden recalled the location of the bank and approached it from the end of Lacour Street, slowing to a fast walk so as not to attract too much attention, although the street now seemed to be empty.

His tension was great, although his plan of action was set. He and three of his men, Hiller, Bentley, and Hoch would enter the bank and demand all the cash on deposit.

Parrett, Slack, and Snyder would remain outside to guard against interference and to hold the horses.

It was just as the first four dismounted that Hiller caught sight of the headline on a copy of the *Record* displayed out front: ARMY CAPTAIN LEADS FORCE TO DESTROY DESERTERS!

"Chrissakes! Sarge," Hiller said, "Look at that!" Madden looked to where he was pointing.

"That army captain has got to be Falk," Hiller said.

"I've been expecting that," Madden said.

"What we going to do now?"

"You don't see him anywhere, do you?" Madden said. "We're going to rob the bank."

He led the way toward the entrance. It was just past noon.

Lone Horse and his Indians came through a pass in the hills a couple of miles north of Pioche.

It was then that he saw the five uniformed cavalrymen, with what appeared to be a civilian scout, riding in from the east, directly below them.

Even as he spotted them, they veered southward, riding fast toward the town.

Tempiute Jim, riding beside him, saw them, too.

"First blood," Tempiute Jim said. "Let us begin."

Lone Horse resented his words, but he raised a fist in signal to his warriors, and motioned downward.

Within minutes the horde was charging down the slope.

Lone Horse had previously spoken to them, cautioning that their initial assault on the town be a silent one. "We will surprise the whites," he'd said.

Now, grimly, he realized the futility of his instructions, hearing the younger braves break out in war cries.

The mounted soldiers below looked up, startled, then instantly spurred their horses into a dead run for the town.

The interior of the bank was empty of customers.

Near the front were two clerks busy with paperwork behind their teller windows. Farther back, at a desk in an open space, a cashier-manager was similarly occupied.

And behind the latter was the door of a walk-in steel vault.

The scene, Madden thought, was as described by the derelict bank robber back there in Chisco. The old bastard hadn't been lying.

Madden grunted something to Bentley and Hoch, and each stepped up to confront a teller at his cage.

Madden and Hiller continued on toward the cashier, who at that moment looked up to see them approaching.

His eyes widened as he took in the half-masked faces, and he made a reflexive motion of his hand toward a drawer.

Madden jerked out his revolver and fired a shot over the cashier's shoulder. It struck the steel door of the vault with a clang, and the cashier jerked his hand from the drawer as if he'd touched something hot.

"None of that!" Madden called, and shoved his way through the spring gate of a surrounding counter, his weapon now aimed at the cashier.

Hiller followed.

Up front, the two clerk-tellers, covered by Bentley and Hoch, had jerked their stares in the direction of the gunfire and stood transfixed.

Madden said to the cashier, "Open the vault!"

The cashier, a man of medium build and age, strongly featured, seemed to regain his nerve. He said, "I can't, it has a time lock."

"At this time of day?" Madden said. "Don't be foolish."

The Chisco derelict had warned him that bank robbery victims always tried to take refuge behind the time lock alibi.

The cashier seemed to see the futility of arguing the point. Still, he made no move to get up from his chair. Instinctively, he stalled.

He said, "You're that deserter bunch, aren't you? The one's been raising so much hell lately."

"You want to see a sample of it, just keep mouthing off," Madden said.

Reason must have returned to the banker then, because he got up, moved quickly to the vault door, and swung it open. Inside was a large safe with a combination lock.

Madden gestured with his revolver. The cashier looked at him, hesitating.

Madden cocked the weapon; the cashier lost his hesitation, bent swiftly, and began to manipulate the dials. In his nervousness he worked the tumblers wrong and had to begin over. Sweat had broken out on his brow.

A short time later he looked up at Madden, saw the uselessness of further protest, and swung open the safe door.

"By God!" Hiller said. "Maybe this is the United States Mint!"

The open door revealed many stacks of currency, in packets of varied denominations. Hiller unfolded a rucksack he was carrying.

"That damn drunk knew what he was talking about,"Madden said. Then to the cashier, "Empty it all out."

Reluctantly, the cashier began to remove the packets, dropping them into the sack as Hiller held it open.

"How much is there?" Madden said.

"Seventy thousand," the cashier said. "A lot of it payroll money. The miners of this town aren't going to like this."

"We've learned to get along without friends," Madden said. "Hurry it up, if you want to live to explain to them what happened."

The cashier hurried, but he was still a man of nerve, and when he dropped the last packet into the sack, he said, "Word is out they've got an army detail on your trail at last. You may not live to spend this, friend."

"Who knows?" Madden said.

He signaled toward the front of the bank, and Hoch and Bentley started herding the two tellers toward him.

They gathered at the vault, as he and Hiller stepped out.

The cashier tried to follow, but Madden stopped him. Madden said to the tellers, "Get in there with him."

When they balked, Bentley and Hoch shoved them in, and Madden slammed the vault door shut and locked it.

The trapped men yelled their protests, their voices loud enough to be heard.

Madden yelled back. "Keep hollering. Somebody will stop by and hear you and let you out."

Hiller, nervous now, said, "Let's go, Sarge, before somebody does come."

Madden led the way out. He looked up and down the street. Several doors south, near the intersection of Main, he saw a few people moving about, in and out of the business structures.

He said to Hiller, "Hold the sack while we stuff the money in my saddlebags."

Slack spoke up then. "We ought to split it up now."

"Are you crazy? Here in the open?"

They got all of it into Madden's bags and mounted up.

"How much?" Slack said.

"Seventy thousand," Hiller said, his elation showing.

"Ten thousand apiece then," Slack said. He was holding a hard stare on Madden.

Madden stared back and said, "That's the way I figure it."

He kicked his horse then, about to lead up to Lacour to the north.

That's when they saw the riders coming. Six of them.

Hiller said, "Them's army, Sarge! And maybe Falk out front."

Madden halted. "Prepare to fire!" he said.

They drew their weapons.

"Ain't that Craig up front with Falk?" Hiller said.

Madden made a quick countermand. "Hold your fire!"

Slack said, "Goddammit! Make up your mind."

"Look behind, Sarge, Hiller said. "They got Injuns chasing them. A whole goddam nation of them, looks like."

Slack said, "Hell, them Injuns won't tell us from them they're chasing." He wheeled his mount. "Let's run for it." He started for the main part of town.

The rest, including Madden, followed.

Too late Madden thought they might have done better to have taken refuge in the bank. As they raced toward Main Street, they could hear rifle fire behind them and the sporadic cries of the Indians closing in on Falk's cavalrymen.

And on Craig, Madden thought.

The men on the streets of Pioche could now hear the shooting and the war cries, and were alerted.

Those walking about with guns on their hips formed an irregular line facing the direction of the sound, not yet fully comprehending what was coming, but instinctively forming a defense against any band of yelling Indians.

As the deserters turned into the intersection, the townsmen let them come. With the yellow neckerchiefs dropped from their faces, although still tied around their necks, they did not yet register that identity on the excited Piochens.

If they were white men, they must be allies, was the first impression.

Then the riders had gone past, and it was too late to reconsider. They had gone by, heading west up Main toward the mining heights. And the armed civilians were now concerned with the five cavalrymen and their guide, who appeared before they could give thought to their predecessors.

There was confusion as Falk, seeing the gunmen's defense, halted his squad to join them. The rushing Indians did not slow until a surprise barrage from the whites hidden among the buildings stopped them. Stopped them in a screaming, squealing pile of wounded, dying warrior and horse flesh.

Those still mounted wheeled about and fled out of range to parley.

It was then that this first bunch of reckless young braves noted that Lone Horse had split off part of his force and led them up the heights to take positions above the main part of the town, and some of these were now firing from a flat-topped hill. It was these who halted Madden's flight toward the high ground of the mines. Halted him and drove him back before he and his men had reached the slopes.

The Indians now had the town caught in a pincer of assault fire, one low and one high. One faced by the townsmen and Falk's troopers, the other faced by Madden and his deserters. Since the town was nearly surrounded by high-rising terrain on three sides, Lone Horse now held the citizens hostage, despite his losses on the initial charge.

Even as Madden fell back almost to where Falk's troopers, sided by the townsmen, awaited another attack, the Indian force on the heights began raking everything in sight with withering fire.

Madden dropped back even farther, now seeking cover among the wooden business structures, realizing at present there was no open route of escape.

They had a hell of a force, he thought. More Indians in

one bunch than he had seen since he had last fought off a war party of Tonto Apaches.

There was increased fire from the citizen defenders, and from his position a couple of doors up the street, he could see the start of a second charge of the Indians.

Instinctively, he pointed at the attackers and gave his men the order to fire.

The addition of this firepower had its effect. The charge slowed, faltered, then turned into a rout. The Indians fled, leaving another strew of casualties in their wake.

Now some of the defenders, seeking to pinpoint their unexpected allies, glanced across the intervening distance.

The deserters, suddenly aware of the attention they were getting, fidgeted under it.

Hiller said to Madden, "We maybe made a mistake here, Sarge."

Madden was having the same thought. A thought brought home sharply as he glimpsed Falk peering from the corner of a mercantile.

Falk stared at him in shocked surprise.

Madden met his stare and held it. In an aside to Hiller, he said, "There's Falk. If he turns his men on us, open fire."

"Just so," Hiller said.

Men of both factions were now peering at each other across the space. It was a moment ready to explode.

Then Falk called, "If they overrun us, we all die."

Madden did not answer.

Falk called them, "I'm asking for first things first, Sergeant. Will you agree to that?"

Slack heard and said, "The hell with him! Let the Injuns take him."

"I'm thinking of us," Madden said.

"Well?" Falk called.

Slack cursed.

Madden hesitated. He looked out beyond carbine range and saw the Indians massing again. Despite their initial losses, there seemed now to be more of them than before. It was a sometimes Indian tactic to make early probing attacks to feel out an enemy's strength. Their next would be the big one, he thought.

It could be the one that would overwhelm the defenders. The one that could make the people of the town victim of Indian blood lust, now aggravated by the Indian's losses.

It was not this thought, though, that decided him. Rather it was impulse, based on his years of experience as an Indian-fighting noncom. With some reluctance, he nodded. And called, "All right, Captain. First things first!"

For a long moment Falk held his eyes, probing him, as if not certain he could believe him.

Finally though, he returned the nod and turned back to face the forming assault party.

And not too soon, for now they came racing in on their third and heaviest attack.

An attack that proved to be little more than a feint.

For as the defenders opened fire, the attackers wheeled and withdrew unscathed, twisting on their mounts to make obscene gestures at them.

At that moment Madden, and Falk too, realized the action here had ceased to be the main point of assault and was merely a diversionary offensive to occupy the defenders.

Because now they could hear the exchange of sporadic fire from the back reaches of the town as other townsmen took up rifles to combat an increased rain of fire from the heights.

The Indians below formed up just out of rifle range, but in plain sight, so as to maintain their posing threat while establishing a holding line across the roads leading from the town.

It appeared to Madden that whoever was commanding them had decided to hold the exit and to rely on his forces above to rain disaster on the now aroused and fearful towns-people.

Those in the back reaches fought back, of course, but with

little effect, as the enemy above, especially on the flat-topped hill, had found cover on its brow from pushed-up rocky soil, left after a potential mining site had been roughly graded, then abandoned.

It was the spot most protected from answering fire from below, and it was now a source of casualties among the citizens taking refuge in the wood structures, as randomly fired shots pierced the flimsy constructions.

It was Falk who saw the big picture first and risked himself to approach Madden where the latter still crouched with his deserters.

Madden had to grudgingly admire the man's audacity for this. The deserters wore bitter scowls as they watched.

"Sergeant," Falk said, "look above and see the major threat. From that hill in particular the red bastards are raining death. There are women and children in this town. And they are even now being killed."

Madden looked, and saw it was so. He also saw that past the hill wound a roadway leading to a gap in the rounded peaks beyond. A roadway that could mean a route of escape for him and his men, were it not for the Indians.

An escape, possibly, without a confrontation and killing of the Fort Halleck soldiers. And this was his desire, to avoid such slaughter, since he believed such an act could bring the hatred of the entire frontier army, once word of it spread throughout the country.

It was something he did not want, especially now that he had a fortune in his saddlebags with which to start a new life.

What Falk said next surprised him.

"Sergeant," Falk said, "with your men and mine, we can take that hill."

"Mine and yours?" Madden said.

Falk said, "The townsmen tell me that road through the gap leads to country that can take you anywhere."

"And you as well," Madden said.

"I would allow you a margin of time for escape."

"Hell," Madden said, "we've got you outnumbered. We can take you now and end our worries."

"You kill these soldiers," Falk said, "and the army will never let up. The West itself will not be big enough for you."

Madden was silent, this being similar to his own thoughts.

"There is another thing," Falk said. "I saw you come out of that bank as we fled before the redskins. I trust you got what you went in there for. How much did you get, Sergeant?"

"I'm admitting nothing," Madden said.

"I would guess it was a considerable amount."

"So?"

"With a good lead, and our smaller force, you could get away scot-free."

"You don't believe that," Madden said.

"I'm saying it."

The firing from the hill was sporadic, but telling. And they could hear the cries of wounded citizens below.

That bothered Madden more than he wanted to admit.

But he said, "Your offer isn't good enough, Captain. It will take a guarantee of immunity from further pursuit by you to buy our help."

The muscles in Falk's jaw worked as he considered this, and for a long moment he did not speak.

Finally, he said, "I am a soldier, Sergeant. And I feel a duty to defend the people of this town against a likely massacre. You were once a soldier yourself. Do you not feel an obligation of your former calling?"

Now Madden was silent. His first impulse was to answer, "Hell, no!" But he could not bring himself to do it.

I am a goddam fool, he thought. *But the man is right: I do feel an obligation, so help me God. Once a soldier, always a soldier? Can that be?*

He said, "Will you agree to drop pursuit?"

Falk appeared to find it hard to answer. As if the cost to

him of what he was about to say was more than he could bear. But finally he said, "I will."

Madden said, "Do I have your word as an officer, Captain?"

"You have it, Sergeant."

Madden looked then at the long slope up to the top of the hill. There was a haze of gunsmoke at the top as the enemy maintained their irregular fire.

He thought, *They are waiting to see if we will charge them.*

He turned then to his men and said, "You heard the captain. We go up that hill. Once we take it, we keep riding on. Free from his pursuit."

It was Slack who spoke first. "You giving orders again? We ain't army no more."

"Stay here, then," Madden said, "and take your chances."

"What about my share of the bank money?"

"It goes with me," Madden said.

His words stopped some of the others who were about to grumble.

"What if you don't make it?" Slack said.

"That's the chance you take. We're going to take that hill, Slack. One way I know you'll be with me is I've got the money."

"That ain't fair," Slack said.

"Maybe so," Madden said. "But that's the way it is."

Then he said to Falk, "You understand, Captain, we make this a mounted charge."

"Agreed," Falk said.

Madden turned now to Craig, who had been a silent listener to the parley. "You with us, Raymond?"

"Just to the top of the hill," Craig said.

"That's good enough," Madden said, and turned back to Falk. "When you're ready, Captain." He would not bring himself to address him as "sir."

Falk said, "Skirmish line. Spread out. Prepare to charge!"

* * *

They were under fire as soon as they hit the upward slope.

Luckily the Indians were notoriously poor shots. But they were armed with an assortment of rifles, and in this mounted charge the troopers' carbines were of little use. They had to reach revolver range to be effective.

Seasoned cavalrymen all, Madden's men spurred their horses to close the distance as quickly as they could, pinning their hopes on the poor aim of the enemy. Concentrating, they reached near enough to open fire at last, not noticing that Falk and his troopers seemed to have dropped behind.

Only Craig was still in the now ragged skirmish line.

At this point they had not yet taken a casualty.

But now, at the close range, the Indian fire was increasingly accurate.

And someone in command at the top of the hill shrewdly directed that fire. The horses began to go down, throwing the riders, or being abandoned by the riders as they sank.

It was Madden, whose mount went to its knees, and who got free of his stirrups and grabbed loose his Spencer from its boot, who shouted to the others, "Carbines!" and hoped they heard.

They did, or if they didn't, were aware enough under fire to do so on their own.

So that the troop, all of them afoot except for a still-mounted Slack, continued on with a dismounted charge, taking advantage of an increasing cover of large boulders.

None of them noticed that Slack did not follow, but instead spurred to where Madden's horse lay dying on its side.

He dismounted, and holding the reins in one hand, tore at the visible saddlebag and withdrew from it a large packet of currency.

Falk, several yards below, and no longer advancing with his Halleck troopers, saw this and knew it was part of the robbery loot. Falk raised his revolver, took a careful aim, and shot him dead.

At that moment, Craig, up in the strewn boulders and

near Madden, raised himself to advance and was knocked down by the enemy fire.

Madden, out of the corner of his eye, saw him fall, and, enraged, arose to rush openly and reach the next scant protection, his remaining five men covering him with a volley from their carbines.

Two of them followed quickly, and now joined him in another volley that allowed the other three to advance.

Madden barked his orders as the deserters worked their way upward, firing now in three-man alternate volleys at the rim of the hill where the Indians lay hidden except for the glints of their rifle barrels poking over, or for a quick glimpse of a warrior rising with a taut bow to send an arrow down at them.

Then up again to dash forward to another sparse rock cover and fire again.

There had been long-range fire from the men down in the streets of Pioche, targeting on the rim of the hill, but as Madden neared it, the bullets stopped, the riflemen fearful of hitting him and his men if they continued their sniping.

We're on our own now, Madden thought, and wondered where that bastard, Falk, was. And, in one sharp moment of bitterness, he knew.

And Craig was down, dead or wounded, and that was another bitterness, but of a different kind.

Craig, who had been beside him, showing the stuff he was made of, showing what a fine soldier he could have been if it hadn't been for that goddam Falk.

And now, with his remaining men, he was struck by the sudden wonder of what he was doing here. Of why he was almost to the top of the hill with its force of entrenched Indians waiting to kill him.

That's what came from the years of experience of fighting Indians. It was the job you were trained to do.

As they drove upward, the Indian bullets whined off the rocks, and bits of gravel stung Madden's face. He gave a quick, sweeping glance around him to tally the men who were still with him.

Hiller, Snyder, Parrett, Hoch, and Bentley drove forward, firing. Then Hiller went down, although Madden, out in the lead of the rush, had no knowledge of it.

Suddenly, Bentley's war cries were stilled, and the charge went on now with only the sound of the gunfire and the pound of cavalry boots digging into the rocky soil of the slope.

Madden still led, but a pace or two behind him, spread out in a short line, came Snyder, Parrett, and Hoch. Hoch grimaced in pain at every step.

When they reached the rim, Madden threw himself over it, his carbine firing, knocking down a crouching brave with the last shot left in his Spencer.

Another rushed him, carrying a hatchet, and he realized then they too were short of ammunition.

He grasped his carbine like a club and laid its barrel alongside the attacker's temple, and the attacker dropped senseless, but still holding the hatchet. This one, Madden thought, had the look of a chief.

There were six or eight dead Indians lying about and others critically wounded.

And there were five of them alive, unhurt. Two of these triggered empty rifles. Both went down from shots from Parrett.

Two of the other three fired in panic, and one missed. The other killed Snyder, and was killed by Hoch.

That left two still on their feet. One aimed at Hoch, and in an exchange of fire, they dropped each other.

The last Indian standing was armed with a bow, and Madden rushed him, making a grab for it, and took an arrow almost through his chest, just below the breastbone.

Hoch, barely alive, and bleeding from both chest and groin now, managed to raise his weapon and kill the bowman.

Madden had twisted as he fell, landing chest down, snapping the protruding arrow. Even so, the vitality of the man caused him to raise his head, and for one brief moment he stared down the slope, as if weighing the value of its climb, and then his head fell forward, burying his face in gravel.

The Fort Halleck cavalrymen withdrew from the assault by order of Falk. They waited with him below, somewhat bewildered by his behavior.

But now Falk, studying the slope, and judging the battle for the hill was over, left them and rode to where Slack's body lay beside Madden's dead horse. Slack's hand still clutched the packet of currency.

Falk looked down and saw the opened saddlebag, with another packet half-fallen from it, and he had his own moment of greed.

But it passed. Whatever he was, he was not a thief.

But, engrossed in this brief temptation, he failed to see a surviving Indian come darting down from the hilltop, through the rocks, to leap over the still body of Craig.

Craig regained clear consciousness and saw the Indian reach Falk, unnoticed, and bring up a hatchet, ready for a downward swing at the crouching officer's head.

Craig's carbine lay stretched before him, still at hand, in the sprawled position in which he had been knocked around and fallen. Somehow he grasped it, sighted it on the Indian's back, and pressed the trigger.

The brave went down, the swung hatchet losing force but striking Falk's shoulder enough to topple him.

And as Falk fell, he glanced upward and met Craig's eyes, and knew what had happened. A strange expression came over his face.

Craig saw it and shook his head, even as he struggled to his feet, feeling the intense pain of a wound in his thigh. He staggered down to Falk.

The Indian was dead, blood pouring from the wound in

his back. There was also a great swelling over his left temple from the blow delivered by Madden's carbine club.

Falk's men from Halleck came up then, and one said, "That blow to the head must have done something to his brain, the crazy way he run down that hill with only a hatchet."

But another one was staring at the body, and said, "By God! That's Chief Lone Horse, hisself! It was him, then, that was leading this raid."

"He won't lead no more."

"No," the other said, "he won't." He paused, then said, "If he's dead, I guess the rest of these Injuns will be pulling out. That's the way they do most often."

Craig stood a few paces away and looked at the deserters' bodies lying dead on the slope.

He said to Falk, in a bitter voice, "Madden and his men are dead, Captain. That should satisfy you."

"But it doesn't," Falk said plaintively. "There's no satisfaction at all."

Craig limped away from the bloodbath. In time the wounds to his body would heal, but those to his spirit still had a way to go.

EPILOGUE

THIS story is fiction, although Pioche was considered at the time to be one of the wildest and toughest mining camps in the West. It still exists as a tourist town.

The Deserter Troop never existed. And there never was a major Indian attack on Pioche. But, under Chief White Horse of the Gosiutes, the attacks on the stations of the Overland Stage Company were real enough to become known in Nevada history as the Gosiute War.

If you have enjoyed this book and would like to receive details on other Walker Western titles, please write to:

Western Editor
Walker and Company
720 Fifth Avenue
New York, NY 10019